Katelyn's Friendship

Katelyn's Friendship

A Novel

Kirsten L. Klassen

FIRST MENNONITE CHURCH
RICHMOND, VA

KATELYN'S FRIENDSHIP
Copyright © 2012 by Kirsten L. Klassen, Elkhart, Indiana 46514
Published on demand. All rights reserved.

ISBN: 978-1-4699-8197-0

Printed in the United States of America
Cover design by Sans Serif, Inc.

This book and the first of the series, *Katelyn's Affection*,
are available through Amazon.com.
To contact the author, email scrabblewiz@yahoo.com.

For my girlfriends,
  all of you,
    and each of you

Katelyn's Friendship

CHAPTER 1

Rachel raised an eyebrow as she handed the phone to her sister Katelyn. "It's Noah Graham, calling from California. I told him he was missing winter here in Indiana." She plopped down on the floor beside her boyfriend Jason and turned back to the television. On this Friday night early in February, the girls had invited their boyfriends, Jason and Shawn, to their house to celebrate the good grades they had received on their report cards earlier that week. Mom was also home, sitting at the dining room table with her friend Max, who was trying to teach her how to play backgammon.

Katelyn realized her surprise must have shown because Shawn, who had been sitting by her on the couch, whispered, "Who's that?" as she stood up to take the call.

"Leah's older brother," she said, stepping over Shawn's feet. Leah was Katelyn's best friend.

Shawn nodded.

"I'll be right back," Katelyn whispered, holding her hand tightly over the receiver to prevent Noah from hearing her. "I'll try to make it quick."

Katelyn started up the stairs, heading for her bedroom for some privacy, then spoke, "Hello? Noah?"

"Hi, Katelyn. I wasn't expecting to reach you on my first try. Leah said you are spending Thursday and Friday nights at your dad's."

"So you were hoping to leave me a message?" Katelyn was restless, wanting to go back downstairs and join the others.

"No, I was going to ask your mom for his phone number."

"He's away . . . presenting a paper at a conference," she said. "We're going to see him Sunday night."

"Well, I'm glad I caught you. I need to talk to you." Noah's voice was deeper than most young men's, and tonight he sounded especially serious.

"Well, I figured that's why you called." Katelyn leaned against the door in her bedroom. "I'm sure this is costing you a fortune. Could you get to the point?"

Noah's voice was cold and deliberate. "Yes. The point. Sorry. The point is . . . you and I need to put aside our differences for Leah's sake. Can you do that?"

Katelyn sat down on her bed, took a deep breath, and said in a gentler voice, "I'm sorry. I didn't mean to be rude. What's the matter?" What could Noah know about his younger sister that Katelyn didn't already know? She had just seen Leah yesterday.

"I can't make this quick," he said.

She winced. "You heard that?"

"Yeah."

"Sorry. I can talk now. The movie we are watching is about halfway through, so I've got some time." Even while Katelyn offered Noah her time, she couldn't imagine what they would find to talk about for an hour. She still hoped this call would be over soon so she could get back to her date with Shawn.

"Leah's not there tonight, is she?" Noah sounded uneasy.

"No. Mom, Max, Shawn, Rachel, and her boyfriend Jason."

"Isn't Rachel a little young to have a boyfriend? She's what, thirteen?"

"Well, maybe 'boyfriend' is too strong a word. Is this really important to discuss right now?" Katelyn wanted to talk about Leah. Why was it always so hard to talk to Noah?

"You're right. That's not important. I'll get to the point. Katelyn, what I'm about to tell you is a secret. You can't tell anyone. No one. Ever."

"Noah, you're making me nervous. Just tell me what this is about."

"Promise first," Noah insisted. "You and I are her best friends in the world." This was, in fact, the reason for the tension between them. They were jealous of each other. But Noah said it now purposefully, as if persuading Katelyn to join his team.

"Okay," she said. "I promise."

"Leah's pregnant."

"But . . ." Katelyn said and stopped immediately. But what? The Leah she had seen just yesterday had dark circles under her eyes, appeared to be losing weight, and had seemed preoccupied. More than once, Katelyn had to remind her it was her turn in their chess game, even though Leah barely took her eyes off the chess board.

She shook her head. "But, Noah, she can't be.

She hasn't seen Carter since Rachel's ballet performance a few weeks ago when he violated the restraining order—and he's been in jail ever since. But they haven't been alone since December when he first beat her up and we took her to the hospital." And, besides, Katelyn told herself, even without these practicalities, even if she was alone with him, Leah wouldn't have had sex with Carter. She had been more adamant than Katelyn about waiting until she was married.

Noah was silent, giving her a chance to catch up.

December? If Leah had gotten pregnant then, she would be just about two months pregnant now, Katelyn realized.

"Oh, no," she whispered. She rubbed her forehead with her hand. "Is it really true?"

"Yeah. It stinks," Noah said. "It's hard to believe they . . . had sex the same day he beat her up. But she thinks that's when it happened."

"Has she told your parents?" Katelyn asked. She could not imagine how Ginger or Pete would react to the news of their daughter's pregnancy.

"No. She can't tell them," Noah said this as if it were true, rather than just Leah's or his opinion. "She says she's put them through enough already, and she can't deal with their reactions. And, she won't tell Carter either. It's not safe for him to know. She's only told me, and now I'm telling you. We are the only ones she wants to know."

Katelyn frowned. "But Noah, it's only a matter of time before everyone knows."

"You're assuming she's having the baby," Noah said quietly. "She's not."

"She's having an . . . abortion?" Katelyn's stomach began to churn uneasily.

"Yes."

"But, Noah, she can't." How could her best friend have an abortion? Didn't she and Katelyn believe the same things?

"Katelyn!" Noah raised his voice, causing Katelyn to jump. Then, through clenched teeth, he said, "Get a grip. This isn't about you. And, it's not about what you think is right or wrong. Leah needs you."

"What for?" she asked.

"I sent Leah the money, Katelyn. All she needs from you is a ride to the clinic in Michigan since she can't drive after the procedure. I looked it up online. It's not far, about forty-five minutes from your house." Katelyn and Leah lived in a small town in Northern Indiana, just a few miles south of the Michigan border.

She was quiet, trying to think. She couldn't seem to focus on one thought at a time. She felt bombarded with thoughts and feelings, one feeling in particular kept taking over—panic.

"So, will you drive her?" Noah asked, after giving her a moment.

Katelyn shook her head no. "I can't, Noah."

"Now I understand why Leah didn't want to tell you herself," Noah muttered.

"Now I remember why I don't like you," she flung back.

"Well, like me or not, Katelyn, we have to find a way past our differences to help her. She needs us. She's got no one else to turn to."

It was true, Katelyn thought. Leah was closest to Noah and Katelyn. Clearly, she had been close enough to Carter to share things with him she had not shared with the other two. But Carter had proven he could not be trusted. And, in this situation, Katelyn was not sure she could come through for Leah.

"Katelyn, I forget this is all new to you. You probably need some time. How about you just think about it? I'll call you back in a day or two, and we can figure out where to go from here?" Noah was asking her now. Katelyn could feel him holding his frustration in check.

"Yeah, okay. But I won't change my mind." She picked at the yarn on the knotted comforter that covered her bed. Then she spoke again, "Noah, is Leah sure she wants to do this?"

"She says she is."

"But maybe if she had more time to think about it?"

"She doesn't have any more time. She's got to decide before she gets to three months." He let that sink in before continuing, "Maybe if this pregnancy had happened in another way or with a different person, she would have made a different choice. I know it would break my heart if Jenna made this choice."

"But you wouldn't, I mean, you haven't. . . ." Katelyn had assumed that Noah and his long-time girlfriend Jenna were waiting to have sex until they were married.

Noah laughed. "Well, obviously, you haven't. But, yes, we have. We've always used birth control religiously—if it's not sacrilegious to say it that way."

"No, I haven't," Katelyn said, her face hot. She did not want to discuss such private matters with Noah, but she was troubled by many things about their conversation, things that went beyond the idea of Leah having an abortion. "I thought we were supposed to wait, Noah. I thought that was how Christians were supposed to live our lives. It's a bit of a shock to discover that no one is."

"Not 'no one' Katelyn," he assured her. "Many people wait."

"But isn't it wrong for us? Aren't we supposed to be different?"

Noah was quiet for a moment, then his voice was reflective. "Katelyn, you're not a child. You know that Christians are as different as the rest of the human race. We believe different things about rock music, homosexuality, how to achieve world peace, the role of women, and yes, even sex. Just because I've had sex . . . been with . . . Jenna doesn't mean I'm not a Christian. I . . . love her. I hope to marry her."

"Hope?" Katelyn was surprised. Though she had not been around Noah much, she knew that marriage between Noah and Jenna had been a plan, not a hope. Noah and Jenna's sense of themselves as a couple had never appeared to waver. When Jenna said she wanted to get away from home for her college education, Noah had willingly agreed. Together, they had chosen a university in California that suited her interests in art and his in journalism.

"It's not as easy as we once thought," Noah said, with a sigh. He sounded tired now, and Katelyn's heart went out to him.

"Well, I hope you can work things out," she said and meant it.

"Thanks. I'll call you in a day or two. Promise me you'll think about what Leah needs from you."

"I'll try." Katelyn ended the call and stared at the phone for several moments. Then, reluctantly, she stood up and went to join the others.

When she slipped back into her place beside Shawn, his arm went easily and naturally around her shoulder, and he whispered to her, "You're back just in time for the credits. Is everything all right?"

She nodded uneasily. She wanted to take him by the arm and pull him into her room and tell him everything she and Noah had talked about. But she couldn't. She had promised to keep a secret that she suddenly felt was far beyond her ability. She knew that Leah would have—and could have—done it for her without hesitating. Leah never told anyone anything. Maybe that was why she had been so good at keeping quiet about how badly Carter was treating her. Leah was made for secrets. But not Katelyn. Keeping secrets had never come easily to her. And, there had never been a bigger secret for her to keep than this one.

After the movie was over, Katelyn walked Shawn out to his car. Jason and Rachel lingered behind in the house, which gave both couples a few moments of privacy. Shawn leaned against the driver's side of the car and pulled Katelyn toward him. He moved toward her and she raised her lips to kiss him, but then his mouth shifted toward her ear and he whispered, "So, what was the mysterious phone call about?"

Katelyn kissed Shawn awkwardly on the cheek. "Noah's worried about Leah." She decided to leave it at that.

Shawn nodded. "And, how is Leah doing?"

"It's still pretty rough for her," Katelyn said, sighing.

"Maybe she'll feel better after she's faced Carter in court?"

"I think we'll all feel better then. But that doesn't seem to be happening anytime soon." She shuddered. "And, how are you doing?" she asked, changing the subject. "I mean, how did it go with your counselor?"

He shifted away from her. "Honestly?"

"No, tell me a lie," she said, laughing.

"Well, then, it's fine, fine. Couldn't be better. He thinks I'm the healthiest teenager he's ever met."

Katelyn reached for his arm and squeezed it. "Okay, now tell me the truth. He hasn't had you committed yet, so it can't be all bad."

Shawn laughed. "No, not yet. And, I am being a good boy and doing as I was told." He was referring to the advice he had received after the fight when Carter had violated the restraining order barring him from seeing Leah. Carter had followed Leah to Rachel's dance performance and tried to get her to leave with him. Shawn had stepped in to protect Leah, and the fight between the boys had escalated. Later Carter threatened to press charges against Shawn, which so far had not happened. But Leah's lawyer had advised Shawn that going for counseling would at least demonstrate remorse and an interest in changing his behavior. Shawn, who had been shaken by the ferocity of his own reaction, had not needed much encouragement. Katelyn had been proud of the way he had spoken to his parents right away, asking for their support, finding a counselor, and scheduling the appointments. Today had been his third appointment.

Now he pulled her closer, sliding his hands under her hair so she felt the warmth of his palm on the back of her neck. "Honestly, Katelyn, it's hard. When I'm there, talking to him, I feel as if there are two of me in the room—and the second me is a very small child."

She waited, thinking he would go on, wanting him to say more. "And?" she asked finally.

"It's a very odd sensation, seeing yourself when you were so helpless. It makes me feel protective and frustrated at the same time."

Katelyn tried to picture herself sitting in a room with a younger version of herself.

Just then they heard the sound of a door opening. Shawn turned toward the house, then back to Katelyn. "I'm still going to need that kiss, even if it is a quick one," he said, leaning down. This time their lips met, and she felt the familiar tingle throughout her body that his kisses inspired so easily.

"All right, all right, haven't you had enough time to say goodnight to your girl?" Jason's voice rang out on the otherwise quiet street. The sound of two sets of footsteps approached the car.

Shawn started to laugh, with his lips still on Katelyn's. She moved away, grinning at him. "Yeah, yeah, I'm coming," he said, opening the car door and sliding in behind the wheel. Katelyn walked around the front of the car to wave goodbye, and noticed that Jason was holding Rachel's hand to his face. He had one arm around her waist, said something quietly which she nodded to, then he kissed the palm of her hand. Katelyn was touched. When Jason let Rachel go, Katelyn saw that her face was shining. As the car pulled out of the driveway, Katelyn moved to stand by her sister.

"There's just something so right about those two brothers," she said, squeezing Rachel's hand and starting for the door.

"You can say that again," Rachel said. "By the way, Mom said she's not getting the hang of backgammon and wondered if we would join her and Max for a game of cribbage."

"You taught him to play cribbage already?" Katelyn was surprised. Her mother had only recently introduced them to Max.

"No, he knew already. Mom said he's really good at games."

"Aren't you worried he'll beat you?" Katelyn asked, grinning as she tugged open the front door.

"Nah. Just looking forward to the challenge of some decent competition for a change," Rachel said.

Katelyn swatted at her. "Well, I'd like to, really I would. But I can't tonight. I've got a short story to read, then I'm going to bed." She felt guilty lying to her sister about something so simple. She had no intention of doing any homework tonight, but she desperately wanted to be alone with her thoughts.

"Aren't you going to join us, Katelyn?" Mom called from the dining room.

"No, not tonight. I'll catch you another time."

"We'd love to have you," Max said.

Katelyn peeked around the corner. "Thanks, Max. But Rachel's really the one to beat. I'll join you another time." Then she turned to Rachel and said, "Good luck."

"Champions don't need luck," Rachel said.

"Humility, then?"

"Oh, go read your story."

Katelyn ran upstairs to her room and threw herself across her bed. She rolled over onto her back and stared at the ceiling. "God," she said, very quietly. "How could you let this happen to Leah? How could you let her be pregnant, after everything else she's been through?"

She lay still for a long time until her vision began to blur and the tears ran down her cheeks. As minute after minute passed, Katelyn became angry. She grabbed her pillow from behind her head and flung it into the air. When it landed on her stomach, she stuffed it into the crook in her arm, twisted onto her side, and muffled her face in her pillow. She let herself cry then, angry sobs. Her body rocked, long after she stopped crying. Finally, sleep came to her.

In the early hours of morning, Katelyn woke with an ache in her heart. Her dreams had been confused, but she had been trying to find something, something she needed desperately before leaving on a trip. She was sorting through closets and drawers, looking for this thing that she couldn't seem to find or name. Everyone was in the car waiting for her, honking the horn. But she couldn't leave it behind and what she was looking for seemed to change as she tore open drawers and cupboards. The sense of loss she felt after waking continued even as she showered and ate breakfast in the quiet house. Mom and Rachel must be sleeping in, she thought as she brushed her teeth. It wasn't until Katelyn opened the front door to a darker and quieter world than she had expected, that it occurred to her to look at her watch. Four-fifteen. Katelyn shook her head and went back inside, plopping down on the couch to watch television until eight-thirty, the time she usually left to get to the Redbud stables, where she volunteered two Saturdays a month.

She did a lot of thinking about Leah in those hours before dawn. When she got to Redbud and her favorite pupil, Kiana, greeted her, Katelyn drew the small girl close in a warm hug. Kiana's respiratory problems usually inhibited her natural energy. But today she was in rare form, her black braids bouncing as she nodded or clapped her hands. Even her feet seemed to be tapping.

"New medication," Kiana's mother said, seeing the question in Katelyn's eyes as she glanced up at her. The parents usually dropped their children off and went to the observation room, but Mrs. Hurley stayed until Kiana had mounted her horse, Trim Jim. "I was afraid she'd take off flying if I looked away." She chuckled then, and patted her daughter's leg. "We have so few days like this, we have to enjoy every moment."

Kiana grinned at her mother. "Time to go," she said, urging her horse forward to join the others in the arena. Katelyn took the halter, and the other volunteer, Pat, moved into position beside Trim Jim to spot Kiana.

The morning passed quickly, and Katelyn was grateful for the reprieve from her thoughts. On the drive home, she caught herself frowning in the rear view mirror. When she got home, she heard loud classical music even before she got inside. She followed her ears to the basement, where Rachel and

Hillary, her best friend, were dancing. Katelyn sat down on the stairs to watch, unobserved. Rachel's long dark hair was pulled back in a braid, and her dark eyes were accented by the black leotards. Hillary also wore black leotards, and Katelyn's eyes were drawn to the contrast of her short blond hair as she swirled and pirouetted among all the brown and black. The two ballerinas were so talented, so graceful, that Katelyn applauded when the music ended.

Rachel took a drink from her water bottle. "Actually, I messed up, but you were probably watching Hillary then," she said.

"You did great, Rach," Hillary said. "I mean, you're so much better than when we first started working on this."

"That doesn't mean I'm getting it right," Rachel said, shaking her head.

"Better counts," Hillary said. "Oh yeah, and don't forget the other thing."

"It's supposed to be fun," Rachel mimicked. Hillary laughed.

"It looked great to me," Katelyn said.

"From someone who knows nothing about dance," Rachel said, then added quickly, "No offense."

"I think I'll make some lunch," Katelyn said. "You interested?"

The girls shook their heads no. "We've got another couple hours of work to do," Rachel said.

"Thanks anyway," Hillary added.

"Maybe you could turn the music down, just a little?" Katelyn asked.

"Sure."

Katelyn went upstairs and made herself a peanut butter and jelly sandwich. Then she got her English textbook and sat staring at the pages, trying to read the assigned short story as she thought about Leah.

In the early evening when the phone rang, Katelyn realized there was one way she could say yes to Noah's request to drive Leah to the abortion clinic. In the short time from the first ring to the third, when she picked up the receiver, she was even able to muster up enthusiasm for what had seemed an impossible request only the day before.

"Hello?" she said.

"Is that you, Katelyn?" Noah asked.

"Yeah. Hi, Noah." Still, she couldn't say yes right away. She was talking to Noah, after all.

"So, what do you think, Katelyn? Will you drive Leah?"

"Yes, I think so," she said.

"You know she'd do it for you in a heartbeat. She'd never even ask you for a reason," Noah said, trying to convince her.

He was right, of course. Leah would do it for her and never even question her. But maybe Leah needed someone to question her, maybe she wasn't thinking clearly.

"I said yes, Noah." Katelyn felt a twinge of conscience. She was letting Noah believe she would help Leah out, but she was going to try to change her friend's mind. She would drive Leah to the clinic, but she was hoping the abortion would never take place.

"Great," Noah said, sounding relieved. "I know this is hard for you. I wish I could take her myself. Thanks, Katelyn."

He wouldn't have said that if he knew why she was doing it, Katelyn thought. In fact, if Noah knew why Katelyn had agreed to drive Leah, she was pretty sure he would have found another way to get his sister to the clinic.

CHAPTER 2

Sunday morning Katelyn's mother had to wake her, she was sleeping so soundly.

"Katelyn, it's eight-fifteen. You need to get up now so we can get to church. We're leaving in forty-five minutes," Mom said, squeezing her shoulder.

In answer, Katelyn opened her eyes and sat up. "Thanks, Mom," she mumbled. She sat there for a few minutes after her mother left the room, hearing her mother's and Rachel's voices, then the two of them going down the stairs, first her mother's heavy steps, then the light steps of her graceful sister.

Katelyn dressed quickly and carelessly, then went to the bathroom and washed her face with cold water. She combed out her hair and pulled it back into high ponytail. Then she went downstairs for breakfast.

"What are we having?" she asked, as she walked by Mom and Rachel sitting at the table.

"Rachel made scrambled eggs. There's some left if you like, but they're probably cold by now," Mom said. The two of them had finished eating, but Mom was still drinking her coffee, and Rachel had left a piece of toast unfinished on her plate. Katelyn reached for it, then looked at Rachel who nodded her permission.

After dishing up the rest of the eggs, Katelyn heated them in the microwave. She took one bite of Rachel's toast, then dropped two more pieces of bread in the toaster. She grabbed the phone and punched in Leah's telephone number.

"Hello?" Leah's father answered.

"Hi, Pete. Can I talk to Leah for a minute?" Katelyn asked.

"Yes, I'll get her. We're on our way out the door. Well, you must be, too." The Grahams' church started at nine-thirty just like Briarwood, the church Katelyn attended with her mom every other Sunday. But the families had different styles: Pete and Ginger liked to get there early so they could sit where they always did, while Katelyn's mom was happy if they arrived before the congregation finished singing the first hymn.

"Yes, I won't keep her long."

"Leah, it's Katelyn," Pete said, muffling the sound with his hand over the receiver. There was one telephone in the Graham's house, and it was not cordless. This was Pete's way of helping his children keep their calls short and to the point, but it also had the unfortunate effect of making it impossible to have a private conversation since the phone was in the dining room.

"Hi!" Leah sounded breathless.

"Hi, Leah. Can you come over after church?" Katelyn asked. She wanted to tell her she had talked to Noah, but she was aware others in both houses could hear them.

"I'll check. Is lunch included?" Leah asked.

"Sure. We'll probably have take-out."

Katelyn heard Leah ask, "Daddy, can I go to Katelyn's after church? Will you drop me off?"

Katelyn smiled in spite of herself. Leah was the only person she knew who still called her father "Daddy."

"He said yes. See you around twelve-thirty," Leah spoke into the phone.

"Okay."

"And, thanks, Katelyn."

She wanted to say she hadn't done anything, but instead, she just said, "Yeah. See you." She felt uneasy that what she intended to do was a far cry from what Noah had asked her to do.

"Bye, Katie." Leah's voice sang the words. She sounded so happy that Katelyn, for an instant, wished she had told Leah she loved her, wished she had done or said something that would have merited the joy of Leah's affection. Any other time, Katelyn would have been as happy to see Leah as Leah was to see her, but on this Sunday, given the conversation ahead of them, she was dreading the meeting with her best friend.

Still, it started out more pleasantly than Katelyn could have imagined. Leah was always a good guest at the Neufeld's and Sunday was no exception.

"How's the dance going?" she asked Rachel.

"It needs work," Rachel said. "I'm going over to Hillary's this afternoon."

"Did you finish your homework already?" Mom asked Rachel.

"Yeah. Oh, Katelyn, don't forget. Dad's picking us up at five to take us out for dinner."

"What about you, Liz? Do you have plans for dinner?" Leah asked Katelyn's mom.

"Why yes. Max has invited me over."

Katelyn watched as Leah chatted easily with her

mother and sister. When they'd finished eating, Katelyn nudged Leah and the two girls went downstairs, where they perched on opposite ends of the worn couch. Leah grabbed a pillow from the floor and held it against her stomach. Her long black curls hung in loose ringlets, down past her shoulders. She looked straight at Katelyn, then away as she said, "I'm sorry I didn't tell you I was pregnant. I didn't know how."

"Yeah, it was better hearing it from Noah," Katelyn said.

"He's been fantastic, you know, through all this," she said. If Leah noticed the anger in Katelyn's voice, she was choosing to ignore it.

Katelyn waited.

"I love, I mean, . . . loved Carter," Leah said finally. Her voice was soft and imploring. "He's not like you think. I mean, yes, he is that way, too. But there is another side to him." Her chin tilted up defiantly, then she went on. "He could be very sweet. He wanted to have a family—his own family. He had been so unhappy in his family growing up. At first, when he talked about having that family with me, I told him I was too young. But he seemed to love me so much, and he could be very convincing. As we got more serious, I began to believe that his dream for us was possible." Leah's eyes took on a faraway look, and Katelyn wondered if that dream still held some appeal.

Leah shook her head, as if to clear it. "But then, things started happening, little things at first. Like when Carter thought he saw another guy look at me. He got angry and accused me of flirting. He doubted I loved him.

"I needed him to know, Katie, please try to understand." Leah's voice was so soft and low her friend had to strain to hear. "It was all so new to me."

Katelyn took a deep breath and reached forward to pat Leah's hand. "Okay, I'm trying." Suddenly she wanted to ask Leah what it had been like to have sex. She pushed the curiosity out of her mind, only to have that thought replaced by another one. What was it like to be pregnant? But she couldn't ask her friend that either.

"I know you are," Leah said. "Otherwise you never would have agreed to drive me to the clinic."

"Yeah, about that," Katelyn said. "What made you decide to have an abortion?"

Leah shifted uncomfortably in her seat. "I can't have Carter's baby, Katelyn. Not now, not ever."

"You mean you won't," Katelyn corrected her.

"If I thought I could disappear and have this baby in some distant place where Carter would never find out—never find me again, and never find the baby—then maybe I could have the baby and give it up for adoption," Leah said, her voice rising in anger. "But I underestimated Carter once, and I won't do that ever again. He hurt me, Katelyn, and he hurt you." She pointed at Katelyn's arm where her sleeve covered the red scar of Carter's knife when she had gotten between him and Leah. "He's not hurting me or anyone I love ever again, not if I can help it. And, I can help it, but not if I'm pregnant."

Katelyn set her jaw, but held her tongue. She realized there was some connection she was missing here, but she heard Leah's determination as much in her voice as in her words. She knew there was no reasoning with Leah now. There would be other times before the drive to the clinic. Maybe she still had a chance.

"So what's the plan?" she asked.

Leah pulled a piece of paper from her back pocket and handed it to Katelyn. "Here are the directions to the clinic. Do you care what day we do this?"

"What do you mean?" Katelyn would have been glad to postpone it as long as possible.

"Do you have any tests coming up or a day when it would be harder for you to get away?"

Katelyn squirmed. "Not Fridays since I'd be at Dad's. His schedule isn't as predictable as Mom's.

Missing school shouldn't be a problem. Even if there were a test, I could make it up since I assume I'll be pretending to be sick, right?"

"That would be the easiest. Sorry to make you lie."

"What are you going to tell your parents?" Katelyn asked. Leah was home-schooled so it would be more difficult to get out of the house for a day without arousing suspicion.

"I want to do some research for a paper I'm working on, and I'd like to explore several of the local university libraries."

"Won't they be surprised you're going somewhere alone?" Katelyn asked.

"Yes. But with Carter in jail, I doubt they'll object. They'll probably see it as a good sign, that I'm not scared to go out on my own. So, I'll call the clinic tomorrow . . ."

"From whose phone?"

"The pay phone at the mall," Leah said. "That will be my first time out by myself. Anyway, I'll try to get an appointment for a week from Monday. If you call me tomorrow night and ask me the right questions, then I can answer without my family wondering what we're planning."

Katelyn nodded. This was not the first time the girls would have played twenty questions to conceal the topic they were discussing. However, she felt suddenly it was the only time that really mattered. Anything they had thought was private before was nothing compared to the magnitude of this conversation.

"And, if someone finds out?" she asked.

Leah's face turned white. "We can't let that happen," she said, balling her hands into fists. "No matter what, Katelyn, you cannot tell anyone. This is so very important. You just have no idea. No one can ever know."

"But. . . ." Katelyn wanted to protest, to remind Leah she was not good at keeping secrets. At the same time, her heart sank. If Leah was this determined that no one should know, Katelyn realized it would be much harder to talk her out of having the abortion.

Leah shook her head. "I know it seems impossible to you. But just do your part and leave the worrying to me. I'm becoming a pro at that, let me tell you." She managed a wan smile.

"Okay." Katelyn said. "I'll follow your lead."

When Dad arrived at five o'clock, Katelyn was more than ready for her friend to leave. After the two girls had finished with their private conversation, Leah had seemed to relax, while Katelyn felt increasingly anxious about what she had committed herself to. She watched Leah sitting in the front seat with

Dad, chatting easily with him, and, for the first time, Katelyn resented Leah's social graces. She wanted Leah to show more emotion about the decision she appeared to have made so easily. She wanted, she realized, for Leah to be miserable, as miserable as she herself was. When they got to the Grahams' house, Leah jumped out of the car and ran around the back of the car to Katelyn's window and stood waiting for her to open it, bouncing back and forth on the balls of her feet to keep warm. In the meantime, Rachel climbed out of the back seat and into the front to sit next to Dad.

Katelyn opened her window a few inches, but Leah motioned her to open it wider. She rolled her eyes, but did it anyway, saying, "Okay Graham, what do you want?"

Leah stuck her face through the open window and kissed Katelyn on the cheek. "I love you, Katelyn," she whispered. Then she ran off, sprinting toward the house, looking for all the world like a girl much younger than her seventeen years, Katelyn thought, watching her go.

When Dad got to the restaurant, he held the door for Rachel to go in first, pausing to wait for Katelyn.

"You were awfully quiet. Is everything okay?" he asked.

She nodded and tried to smile, slipping in the door.

He put his arm around her shoulder. "You know you can talk to me, right? About anything."

"Yes, Dad. Thanks!" She squeezed his hand. She was glad to see him and wanted to enjoy her time with him. "So, did you have fun? At your conference, I mean?"

"Did I have fun? Did I ever!" he exclaimed, as he sat down next to Rachel, who beamed at his enthusiasm. "Well, first they lost my luggage."

"No!" Katelyn said, in disbelief. Her father flew regularly and had bragged about how his luggage had always arrived.

"That's right. This was the trip where the airlines ruined their perfect record for me. Not only that, but since I arrived in the evening, I couldn't go shopping for a suit until the next day, and I had a meeting—a very formal meeting—first thing in the morning," Dad said. In addition to borrowing clothes from his shorter and more rotund friend, Dad talked about how he fell asleep in another colleague's presentation. His own seminar was so full that people were pushing the chairs aside to allow more room for standing. Then the fire inspector for the hotel had shown up, counted the people there, and ordered thirty people to leave since they were violating a fire regulation that restricted the number of people in each room.

Hearing about her father's business trips was one form of entertainment all the Neufelds enjoyed. During these times, the storyteller in Dad came out, and his only goal was to make them laugh. Tonight was no exception, and Katelyn was relieved to find she could put aside her weighty thoughts and just enjoy listening to her father.

After dinner when Dad had dropped them off at home, Katelyn sat on the couch with a novel open on her lap, staring at the pages. Mom and Rachel were bustling around getting their work and school stuff together. When the telephone rang around nine, Katelyn uncharacteristically let Rachel get it without racing to answer it.

Rachel chatted for a few minutes, then walked over to her sister and dropped the phone in her lap, "It's Shawn."

"Hey, Katelyn. How was your day?" Shawn asked warmly.

"Fine. What about yours?" she asked, stretching out on the couch.

"Fine? Fine? C'mon you can give me more than that," he prompted. "What did you do?"

"Went to church, then Leah came over, then we

had dinner with Dad," Katelyn reported. "How was yours?"

"Mine was great. I'll get back to that in a minute. How's Leah?"

Katelyn wasn't sure how to answer. "Leah's still . . . dealing with Carter," she said, trying to answer honestly without encouraging Shawn to ask more.

"Yeah, I imagine that will take time. It's good she has you." He waited, giving her a chance to say more.

"And your day?" Katelyn asked, when she realized he was not going to break the silence.

"We went bowling this afternoon, and that was a blast. I got four strikes in a row, can you believe it?"

"That's nice," she said, absentmindedly. "I mean, I take it that's good?"

"Yeah, pretty good—at least for me. Someday, you know, it's every bowler's dream to bowl a game of all strikes," he said. "How was your dinner with your dad?"

"It was fun. He was full of stories of his trip," Katelyn said. "And, how was church?"

"Pretty good. The sermon was interesting, about how your values are reflected by how you spend your money. You went to church with your mom this week, right?"

"You're doing a good job of keeping track of the schedule," she said.

"Well, I know next Sunday is a special day, since I get to come to church with you and your dad," Shawn said.

"Yeah, what is that again? February 14? I never can remember what we're celebrating," she said, laughing.

"That's because it's not a religious holiday," he teased. "It's just my favorite holiday. At least it will be this year."

"Why's that?" Katelyn asked.

"This is the first year I will actually have a Valentine. So I can see if the day lives up to its hype. You know. Am I loved enough or what?"

Katelyn grinned. She and Shawn had been dating since September, but it was only last month that she had ended her relationship with Nathan, who was away at college. Although she felt sure of her decision, she had not found the right moment to tell Shawn yet. Maybe she would tell him on Valentine's Day.

"Katelyn?" Shawn asked. "Do you want to come over tomorrow night?"

"Sure, that'll work. How about after supper?" she asked.

"Great," he said. "Oh, and save me a seat in English lit, will you?"

"Of course," she said. "See you then."

Katelyn reached for the remote and turned on the television. Mom walked in and sat down next to her. Then Rachel joined them, sitting on the floor to hook a small blue rug.

"Have you finished your homework?" Mom asked Katelyn automatically.

"Yes, Mother," Katelyn answered, imitating a robot's monotone.

Mom looked over and wrinkled her nose at her.

Katelyn tried to smile back, but looked back at the television before her mother could see her heart wasn't in it. Katelyn leaned against her, breathing in deeply the familiar scents of her mother—strawberry shampoo, peppermint gum, talcum powder, and ever-so faintly, sweat. Her mother slipped her arm around Katelyn's shoulder.

Rachel looked up from her project at the two of them, and Katelyn saw a small smile dance across her lips before she ducked her head back down. It was rare in the Neufeld house for their mother to show affection. Mom pressed her cheek on her older daughter's head. Katelyn would have been happy to stay that way until bedtime, but her mother began to fidget and stir all too soon, and finally spoke, "Hot chocolate sounds good to me. Girls, would you like some hot chocolate?"

Katelyn sat up reluctantly. "Sure, Mom. That would be great."

"Me too," Rachel said.

As she watched her mother leave, Katelyn tried to imagine telling her if she were pregnant. She wasn't sure she could have faced her mother's disappointment either. And certainly, Katelyn knew, if she had already decided to have an abortion, it would have been even more difficult to tell her mother. Leah's mother was almost impossible to talk to. Ginger had not known what to do when Katelyn called to tell her they were taking Leah to the hospital after Carter beat her up. Leah's dad had handled the situation better. Pete might be a better parent to help Leah with her pregnancy. But first he would be furious with Carter and might march down to the county jail to give Carter a piece of his mind.

No, Katelyn realized that if she were Leah, she would have done exactly what Leah had done—tell the older brother who had always been fiercely protective of her, had always had a hug for her, and had always insisted on her right to make her own decisions. But right now, Katelyn was convinced he was letting Leah make the wrong decision, and Katelyn had to stop her.

She lay awake thinking a long time Sunday night after she went to bed. Still, she woke up a half an hour before her alarm clock was set. She got up immediately and found her mother in the kitchen, showered and fully dressed, pouring a cup of coffee.

"Mornin', Mom," Katelyn said and kissed her on the cheek. She felt immediately the inadequacy of the gesture. She needed reassurance. She wanted to feel her mother's arms around her again, to hear her say that everything would be all right, to know her mother's love could survive anything she might do or help her friend to do.

"Good morning, Katelyn," Mom said, taking a sip of her coffee. "You're up early."

"Yeah, I was done sleeping, I guess," she said.

"Well, since you have time, do you want me to make you some oatmeal with fruit, nuts, and cinnamon?"

"Sure. I'll just go shower." Katelyn ran up the stairs, pleased at her mother's offer. Mom had cooked a lot less since she'd gone back to work, and although Katelyn understood the reasons for it, she missed her mom's cooking. And, she realized wryly as she got dressed after her shower, she was not above taking some comfort where she could get it. Perhaps oatmeal was the only reassurance she was going to get that everything would indeed be all right.

At school, Katelyn felt she was walking around in a daze. She arrived late to English literature, too late to save a seat for Shawn as she'd promised. As she came in, he waved at her from across the room and tapped his wristwatch to tease her. After school, Katelyn had to take Rachel and Hillary to their dance class, which gave her the perfect time to call Leah to find out when she'd scheduled the appointment at the clinic.

When Katelyn pulled into the parking lot of the dance studio, Rachel and Hillary went running off to change for their class. She followed more slowly, checking out the pay phone in the corner of the lobby. Once the girls were in class, Katelyn dialed Leah's number.

"Hi, Leah? It's me, Katelyn."

"Yeah, it's me. The coast is clear, for a minute anyway."

"Did you get an appointment?"

"Yes, we're on for a week from today, Monday at ten."

Katelyn felt her heart sink.

But Leah kept talking. "I'll pick you up at eight-thirty. That'll give us plenty of time to get there. We should be back by one o'clock at the latest, and I'll leave your house no later than three so I don't run into Rachel."

"Rachel and Hillary have dance class until four-thirty Monday night," Katelyn said. "Mom's not usually home before five-thirty, so you should be okay at this end. But Leah, are you sure you want to take your car? I can drive, if you prefer."

"No, we have to take mine so it will show that I drove a similar distance as if I had gone to the university library. And, I have to get my paper done in advance, and that's going to be hard enough. Is there any chance you could spend an evening with me at the public library this week?"

"Leah, slow down." Katelyn bit her lip and tried to keep up with her friend. "Okay, you're right. We'll take your car. Yes, I can go to the library with you tomorrow. I'll pick you up after school. You can have dinner at my house, and I'll bring you back around nine. That'll give us several hours in the public library. And, Leah, one more thing."

"What?"

"You can change your mind at any time. I've been thinking. I'll help you tell your parents, if you like."

Leah was quiet for a moment, and Katelyn wasn't

sure if she was angry or thinking. "Thanks, Katelyn. I appreciate your offer. But I've had enough time to think about it, and I won't change my mind. This is the best choice I can make, given the circumstances. I'll tell you more later. Not tomorrow, but after it's all over. I understand this is hard for you, Katelyn, but I'm glad you're here for me. There's no one, Katelyn, no one I'd rather have on my side than you."

Katelyn's eyes filled with tears, and she wanted to tell her that she wasn't on her side. She just couldn't take her side on this.

"I'll see you tomorrow, then?" Leah was asking.

"Yeah," Katelyn said, hanging up the receiver. Then she sat down in the lounge and pulled out a notebook. Sighing, she tried to do her homework. After a few minutes, she gave up and went to watch Rachel and Hillary dance.

Later that night, when Shawn came over, Katelyn found it difficult to relax. He had brought Jason along to see Rachel, and the four had played a game of cribbage. Katelyn and Shawn had lost miserably, partly because she wasn't able to concentrate and was playing her cards carelessly.

Then Shawn said, "Let's go for a walk. It's almost warm enough, if we walk fast."

"Good idea," Katelyn said.

"Hey, what about us?" Rachel asked.

"Get Mom to join you for a game. She's been in her study since dinner, doing who knows what. She could probably use a break," Katelyn said, walking away to get her coat and mittens. Shawn was already bundled up and waiting at the door. He handed her a scarf.

"We'll be back in a half hour, if we can stand it that long," Katelyn said, wrapping the scarf around her head.

"We'll miss you," Rachel said, giggling.

As soon as they were out of the house, Shawn slipped Katelyn's mitten off and put it in his pocket with his own. Then he warmed her hand in his, and she smiled at him in the dark.

"Everything okay, Kate?" he asked.

"Yeah, I guess."

"Which really means you're not ready to talk about it," Shawn said. "That's okay. I'm hoping to be around long enough in case you change your mind."

She laughed softly and squeezed his hand.

"So, Katelyn, have you been in touch with Nathan since he went back to school?"

She hesitated. This wasn't a conversation she wanted to have today. But maybe Shawn needed to know. "Shawn, I wrote to Nathan a few weeks ago and . . . broke it off."

He stopped walking and turned to look at her, his eyes opened wide in surprise. "You did what?"

"I ended it."

"Why didn't you tell me?"

"I was waiting for the right time, I guess. It seemed a little awkward to bring up." Katelyn and Nathan had spent a lot of time together in the two years before he'd gone to college in September, but they had never talked about their feelings for each other. Once he had moved to the Kansas campus, he had not contacted her. The silence had been deafening. Katelyn and Shawn had started dating then. At Christmas, when Nathan was home, he was suddenly sure he loved her. But Katelyn was drawing closer to Shawn, and her feelings for Nathan had changed.

Now Shawn was quiet. They were still holding hands, and Katelyn felt a tremor go through him. "What's the right time for good news, Kate? Why was it awkward to tell me something you know I'd been waiting to hear?" His voice was hurt. He started walking again, as if he wanted to walk away from her, but he was still holding her hand.

Good news, Katelyn thought as she hurried to keep up. Yes, that was how he would see it. She had thought of it that way at first, before she understood she could not shrug off Nathan's loss or her own sense of having lost a friend.

"I was going to tell you Sunday after church," she stammered. She could not say Valentine's Day, like she'd intended. But Shawn looked at her and nodded.

"I ruined your surprise," he said, understanding.

"It's okay. I'm glad you know now."

"What did he say? I mean, after he got your letter?"

"He didn't say anything. He just stopped sending e-mails and calling."

"I don't get it. I mean, are you sure he got your letter? And, if he did, after all the time you two were involved, why didn't he at least respond to your letter?"

Katelyn was getting frustrated, and it showed in her voice. "How should I know? What would you expect him to say? 'Got your letter. Doing fine. No longer wishing you were here.' Or maybe 'Your wish is my command?' Or 'Ouch, that hurt.'" She shook her head. "Maybe he just doesn't have anything to say right now. I'm sure if he did—if he does want to say something, he'll bring it up."

"So, you're relieved, then? I mean, that he hasn't said anything?"

She frowned. "Yeah, I guess so. Is that cold?"

"Well. I don't know the situation. I can't believe the guy went off and left you last fall without staying in touch with you—I mean, he must have been going through something major. But I'll tell you this, Katelyn, if you date me for two years and then you want to break up with me, I hope you have the respect for me to do it in person."

"What's the difference?" she asked, curious.

"A good relationship is like a good conversation," Shawn said. "We take turns talking and listening, not because it's just good manners, but because we care about what each other has to say. Sometimes, when people write letters, they're just dumping their words on the other person, not caring what the other person thinks or how he feels."

Katelyn looked up at Shawn, his face lit up by a street light. "Oh, I see," she said. "One of your girlfriends broke up with you by letter."

"No," he said. "It was me who wrote the letter. And, boy, did she set me straight."

CHAPTER 3

On Tuesday at the library, while Leah worked feverishly on her paper, Katelyn was able to catch up and work ahead on her own schoolwork. She had resolved to try to enjoy Leah's company, without pressuring her—for now. On Thursday, she stopped by the Graham's house on her way home from school, just to see for herself that Leah was okay. Katelyn realized her anxiety about her friend was not entirely rational, but she felt the need to see her or hear her voice almost every day. Once she was with Leah, she was able to relax. She was quieter than usual, but Leah did not seem to mind. In the past, one or both of them might have felt it was necessary to fill the silence with jokes. Now, they were content to be together. Katelyn felt they had rediscovered a way of being together that was familiar to them, before they had boyfriends.

Still, by the end of the week, Katelyn knew her teachers were becoming concerned that something was wrong. No matter what she did, she could not make it to any of her classes on time. By Friday, two of her teachers had made her stay after class to discuss the problem, and a third had suggested that Katelyn make an appointment with the guidance counselor. So far, it had been only a suggestion, but Katelyn knew if she could not improve, she would wind up in the counselor's office to discuss the "underlying problem." Previously, Katelyn had always been on time, so her behavior was all the more noticeable. Even Shawn had asked her if her watch was keeping time correctly. Katelyn had glanced down at her watch, then blushed because it was the gift Nathan had given her for Christmas.

As if she didn't have enough to worry about, Katelyn found herself thinking a lot about whether she owed Nathan a chance to air his feelings about them breaking up. She thought that was why she wore the watch, as an apology. She had even gone so far as to call his dorm one evening after Rachel and Mom were in bed. But Nathan had been out, and she had not left a message.

On Saturday morning, as Katelyn pulled into the parking lot of Redbud, she saw Mrs. Hurley's beat-up station wagon. She checked the time. Eight-forty five. She breathed a sigh of relief. For once she was on time; it was Kiana and her mom who were early.

She found Kiana in the stable with the other volunteer, Pat, and Trim Jim, who was already saddled and ready to go. Pat was holding the horse's reins and talking in a low voice. But Kiana was sitting on a bale of hay, looking unusually tired. Her black hair was pulled back by a simple headband, rather than the tiny braids Katelyn was accustomed to. Dark circles made her eyes appear huge in her small face. But it was her silence that alarmed Katelyn the most.

"Hey, Kiana. How's my favorite rider?" Katelyn asked, trying to sound cheerful.

The girl managed a small smile and put her hand up in a half-hearted wave.

Katelyn looked at Pat, who nodded slightly, sharing her concern.

"She hasn't said a word," Pat said.

"Kiana, are you okay?" Katelyn asked, sitting

down next to the girl and wrapping her arm around her tiny shoulders.

Kiana leaned into her briefly, then stood up, straightening her shoulders. She reached for Katelyn's hand and started pulling her toward the riding arena. Katelyn followed her, then Pat, with Trim Jim bringing up the rear.

Once in the arena, Katelyn turned to whisper to Pat, "Wait for me. I just want to check in with her mom." To Kiana, she said, "Hang on, honey. We've got plenty of time. Class doesn't start for a few minutes. I'll be right back."

Kiana nodded.

Katelyn jogged over to the observation room, where a few parents were gathered. Mrs. Hurley left her place at the window and met her at the door.

"Is Kiana okay?" Katelyn asked.

"Yes, she's fine."

Katelyn frowned. "She . . . she just seems so tired."

"Yes, I know. But she needed to come, Katelyn. She wanted to ride so badly, and she's missed so many lessons these past few months." Mrs. Hurley spoke quietly, with her usual air of dignity.

"But . . . ," Katelyn felt uneasy. "I don't understand. She was so much better last week."

"It has always been up and down, Katelyn. Last Saturday was a great day. Today is a hard day." Mrs. Hurley turned to watch as Pat helped Kiana into the saddle. All of the children were mounting their horses. Class was about to start. Still, Katelyn waited, wanting a better answer.

"Kiana needs to be here today, dear." She reached up, placing her palm on Katelyn's cheek. "She needs you, too. The Kiana you know and love is in there underneath the tired and quiet girl you see today. She's got a nasty sore throat, and she's afraid if she talks, she'll start coughing, and I'll take her to the hospital again. You can talk enough for the both of you today if you set your mind to it."

Katelyn squared her shoulders and turned toward the arena. She walked slowly, trying to compose herself before Kiana saw her, and a song came into her head, one Kiana had sung to her. She greeted Kiana singing about the tiny mouse who painted whiskers on his friend's house. A trace of a smile lit up the girl's face. It was just a small smile, but it was enough to keep Katelyn chattering for the rest of the class. When the class was over, Katelyn carried Kiana to her mother's station wagon and set her down gently. Kiana was asleep before Katelyn had fastened her seatbelt.

Mrs. Hurley's eyes met Katelyn's in the rear-view mirror, and she smiled. Katelyn tried to smile back, but she felt like crying. She hadn't realized before how fragile Kiana really was, and how much strength it took her to face the challenges of her life each day. She kissed the girl's cheek, then backed out and shut the car door. Then she walked around to the driver's window and tapped on it for Mrs. Hurley to open it.

"Would it be okay if I called her or stopped by later this week? Just to see how she's feeling?" she asked. Katelyn had visited Kiana before when she was in the hospital, but never been in the Hurleys' home.

"Sure. She'd like that. Let me write down our home number for you," Mrs. Hurley said, ripping a small corner off a page of the notebook she always carried with her, the book she was writing on her life with Kiana. She handed the paper to Katelyn, who put it in her pocket.

In the early afternoon, when Katelyn left Redbud, she drove straight to Leah's house. Joshua, the quieter of Leah's younger twin brothers, answered the door. He looked at her a bit strangely, then asked, "Is she expecting you?"

Katelyn shook her head no. "I came at the last minute. Is she home?"

"Oh yeah, she's home. She's just doing weird girl things." Then he grinned slightly. "I'll tell her you're here." Joshua slipped past Katelyn up the stairs, where she could hear him knock on his sister's door. She wondered exactly what "weird girl thing" the eight-year-old was referring to.

The next steps Katelyn heard were the heavy steps of a slightly overweight woman coming from Leah's bedroom. Soon Ginger appeared on the stairs, a little out of breath. She called to Katelyn, "C'mon up, Katelyn. Leah's in her room. She doesn't want her brothers to see her just now."

Mystified, Katelyn trotted up the stairs, passing Ginger, who was trying not to laugh. Joshua stood across the hall from Leah's room, trying to catch a glimpse of his sister. Before Katelyn could knock, the door opened quickly and hands reached out to pull her in.

"What's going on?" she started to ask, but then she saw her friend. Leah's face was covered with a green mask, and the towel that covered her head was clearly stained with some type of coloring treatment.

"No way!" Katelyn said gleefully. "How did you get permission to color your hair?" Leah had begged to add maroon highlights to her dark curls for years, but her parents had forbidden it.

Leah looked down, but the corners of her mouth danced. "I think they felt sorry for me," she said, starting to giggle.

Katelyn laughed. "Well, we all feel sorry for you, but we don't all think you should dye your hair red and paint your face green. What will it be next?"

"Yellow contact lenses that glow in the dark," Leah said, trying for a straight face, but losing it.

After Leah had washed off the green mask and rinsed her hair, she said, "I really was only going for the hair, but you know my mom."

Katelyn raised her eyebrows. She wasn't sure what Leah meant.

"She goes in for the whole beauty routine. She got so excited about my hair, I realized it must have been Daddy who had been against it all along. Then she wanted to give me a facial and a manicure." Leah held out her nails to show Katelyn. They were longer than usual and a beautiful dark red. They looked strange. At first Katelyn couldn't figure out why.

"They're fake," Leah offered.

"They don't look like your hands."

Leah looked at them. "No, they don't. They look like a woman's hands."

Exactly, thought Katelyn. That was it, and it

frightened her. She didn't want her friend to grow up and become unrecognizable.

"Leah, I'm scared," Katelyn said, her stomach beginning to ache.

Leah put her arms around her.

"I'm scared of what will happen if you have the abortion. What if they mess it up and something bad happens to you?"

"They're doctors and nurses," Leah said. "They'll take good care of me."

Katelyn wasn't worried only about her friend's physical health, but she didn't say anything. There was still time, she thought, still time to talk Leah out of it.

On Sunday morning, Dad picked up Katelyn and Rachel, and the three of them went to get Shawn and Jason. Katelyn thought Dad had suggested this because he wanted to see where the boys lived. Awkwardly, when they arrived, everyone piled out of the car and up the front steps of the Roberts' two-story brick house. Rachel, who had not seen the house, rang the doorbell eagerly. A cacophony of sound erupted in the house: the voices of several males yelling, a dog barking, a door slamming, heavy feet running down stairs. The door burst open and Jason, dressed in black pants and a white shirt, stood in front of them, grinning from ear to ear.

"Hey, Rachel. Katelyn. Mr. Neufeld," Jason said. "Come on in."

Mrs. Roberts emerged from the kitchen, drying her hands on a dish towel, and began chattering away happily. "Hello, girls. You must be Luke Neufeld. It's a pleasure. I can see where Katelyn gets her height—and her coloring from. I'm Viv Roberts. You've met the boys. And, my husband Jim will be along shortly."

"Good to meet you, too, Viv," Dad said. "Thanks for letting Shawn and Jason join us for church."

"No problem at all," Mrs. Roberts said. She studied him, then, looking as if she would have added more. Katelyn wondered if she suspected that her dad was a little less thrilled with his daughters attending other churches.

"Can I see your dog?" Rachel asked Jason.

"Sure," he nodded, reaching for her hand at first, then, glancing at her dad, he gestured for her to follow him up the stairs. They passed Shawn on his way down.

"Don't let her out, Jason," his mother called. "You know, she'll just come running down and jump all over them." Then to Katelyn's dad, she added,

"Sophie's an English setter, a beautiful creature, really. But she's still a puppy, even after four years."

Shawn grinned his welcome to Katelyn as he passed Jason and Rachel. She smiled back, noticing how handsome he looked in his brown pants, light brown shirt, and matching tie.

"Good morning, Mr. Neufeld," Shawn said, shaking his hand. "Thanks for picking us up and letting us come to church with you." He slipped on his jacket, then stood next to Katelyn. She reached for his hand. His palm was warm and just a bit sweaty. She looked at him, but could see no traces of nervousness in his face as he winked at her.

On the drive to church and after, Katelyn was grateful to her dad for trying to engage the guests in conversation. He did a good job of including everyone. For her part, Katelyn tried not to whisper too much to Shawn, wondering if it felt awkward to Dad that he was the only one without a date. After lunch, Dad dropped all four of them off at Mom's house, where Rachel and Jason took off for the computer room.

Shawn plopped down on the couch. "I like your dad," he said.

Katelyn grinned at him and sat down next to him. "I'm glad. I like him, too."

"Where's your mom?"

"Out with Max. She said she'd be back for supper."

Shawn slipped his arm around her and pulled her close for a long kiss. "Happy Valentine's Day, Katelyn."

"Umm," she said. "It's pretty happy, I think."

"We've been going out for a while now, almost five months, right?"

She nodded against his arm.

"I think you're amazing, you know that?" he asked.

"Yes, I'm amazing."

They both laughed. "You're so comfortable with everyone—my sister, my dad, even the men at the homeless shelter where your mom volunteers," she said. "It puts me at ease, too. You know, it's contagious."

"Thanks," he said. "Katelyn, I know you may not be ready to hear this. But I want to date you and only you. I hope you're getting closer to feeling that way about me."

Katelyn sat still against Shawn for a long moment. She found herself wondering if Carter had said these same words to Leah. Although Katelyn knew Shawn was nothing like Carter, she still felt uneasy. She sat up to face him.

"Shawn, I don't want to date anyone else right now," she began. "I'm happy with you." She wanted to say something else, something to explain her confusion about where exclusivity left off and possessiveness began, the line Leah had failed to notice until it was too late. But when she saw his face light up in response to her words, she simply leaned toward him to kiss him. In that moment, as she gave herself to the kiss and to his joy, she understood something about Leah and Carter.

"Thanks for the perfect Valentine's Day," Shawn said later, when they were saying goodnight at his house. Katelyn had driven the guys home, and Jason had gone in to quiet Sophie.

"See you tomorrow at school," Katelyn said, smiling. It wasn't until she was climbing into her car that she realized she wouldn't see him. She would be with Leah.

When Katelyn's alarm clock went off Monday morning, it was her only proof that she had slept at all. She had been sure she had tossed and turned the entire night, trying on argument after argument to convince Leah not to have the abortion.

Katelyn got out of bed and stumbled down the hall into her mother's room.

"Mom, I don't feel well."

Mom, who was buttoning up her blouse, turned to face Katelyn. "You don't look so great either," she said, reaching out a hand to Katelyn's forehead. "You're a little warm. Where does it hurt?"

"My head mostly, but my stomach's also queasy." Katelyn was telling the truth about the headache, but the rest wasn't true. A headache by itself wasn't usually reason enough to stay home.

Mom sighed, then said, "Well, crawl back into bed. Do you need some aspirin or anything?"

"No, I'll just try to rest first and see if that helps."

Katelyn went back to bed, listening to the sounds of Mom and Rachel getting ready to go off to their normal days of work and school. She wondered what Leah was thinking and feeling. When the door finally slammed shut and the house was quiet, Katelyn climbed reluctantly out of bed, showered, and got dressed.

Leah was late. Eight-thirty came and went without a sign of her. Fifteen minutes of pacing later, Katelyn was beginning to hope Leah had changed her mind about the abortion. She wanted to call Leah, but she knew she couldn't. What if Carter had escaped from jail and gone to see Leah? What if he figured out Leah was pregnant? No, he was in jail. He didn't know anything, Katelyn told herself, pushing away the pictures in her mind of Leah lying dead, covered with blood at Carter's feet.

Finally, five minutes before nine, Katelyn heard the familiar sound of the old Honda's noisy arrival as Leah pulled in the driveway. Katelyn yanked open the front door, pausing only to lock it behind her, and sprinted down the sidewalk to the passenger door, which Leah had pushed open for her.

"What happened to you?" Katelyn demanded, as she fastened her seatbelt. "I thought you said eight-thirty."

Leah nodded, her face pinched as she backed out of the driveway. "Yes. I'm sorry. I couldn't get away any sooner. Mom started asking about the paper I'm working on. She wanted to make sure I knew I was supposed to be writing an argumentative paper instead of a comparative paper, even though the twins are working on a comparative paper now. And, it just went on from there. I didn't know how to break it off any sooner without making her suspicious. Don't worry, though. It should only take us a half hour to get there."

"Or fifteen minutes if you're going to drive with your usual disregard for speed limits," Katelyn said, pointing at the sign indicating they were in a thirty-mile speed zone. She glanced over at the speedometer and saw her friend was going forty-five. "You can't afford to get stopped today."

Leah looked over at Katelyn and grinned. "Are you trying to tell me that my luck's running out?" But she let up on the gas pedal, until the speedometer hit thirty-five. "I knew I brought you along for a reason."

"Which reminds me," Katelyn began. "Are you sure about this?"

Leah knew exactly what she meant. "Yes."

"I keep wishing you'd at least told your parents."

Leah raised her eyebrows. She stared straight ahead for several long moments, then she said thoughtfully. "I wish I had the kind of relationship with them where we could talk about these things. Openly and easily, without them telling me what's right and what's wrong. If they could just listen, like Noah does . . ."

Katelyn wanted just then to tell Leah what was right and wrong, but she recognized that her friend would not be open to hearing her point of view—especially if she expressed it in those terms. Maybe if she asked Leah questions instead, maybe Leah could gradually come to see things differently.

"If you have the abortion, aren't you afraid you'll regret it later?" Katelyn asked.

"For starters, it's 'when' I have the abortion, not 'if.' And, no."

"How do you feel about the . . . baby?"

"Technically, I believe it's an embryo, not a baby yet. But, more to your point, I don't think about it," Leah said, glancing at Katelyn.

When she didn't go on, Katelyn asked, "You don't see it as separate and unique and . . . innocent?"

Leah shook her head no, then added. "I'm sorry. You're asking me fair questions. I feel like the baby is Carter's—completely. And, that part of ending the relationship with him is ending this pregnancy."

"But isn't the baby partly you?"

"You know, on some level, I know it is and that you're right. But I don't feel that way. I feel it's one hundred percent his."

"That's odd," Katelyn said, forgetting her arguments.

"I suppose so," Leah said. "Maybe we can talk about this another time. Right now, I need a little help with directions."

Katelyn realized there was so much she didn't know about her friend. She wanted to know more about what Leah was experiencing, but at the same time, she felt shy and young next to her. She felt as if Leah had outgrown her—that suddenly she had shot up and beyond her into the world of adults. Katelyn reached for Leah's hand, wanting to hold it and pull her back in time. Leah squeezed her hand once, and didn't let go.

The two girls didn't talk again until they reached the clinic. Katelyn was surprised to see it was just a house that had been converted into an office. A sign on the lawn gave the name of the practice, but did not say "Abortions performed here." Katelyn wondered if protesters ever gathered here. It seemed so quiet and ordinary. A few cars were parked in the back lot where Leah parked, and the entrance was on the side.

Leah climbed out of the car and leaned down to look in. "Katelyn, I know you don't like this. But it means a lot to me that you're here. More than you'll ever know."

Katelyn nodded and got out of the car. She had failed. The abortion was going to happen, and there was nothing she could do. She had not known what to say. She still did not know what to say. She was sad and angry and scared all at the same time. Walking beside Leah on the way into the clinic, she wondered what her friend was feeling.

Leah appeared confident as she walked straight to the receptionist's desk and announced herself. Katelyn sat down in one of the corners of the waiting room. She glanced around the room, wondering at the mother with her young daughter, a girl who looked no older than thirteen. A young couple was seated in another corner. The woman had been crying. Her boyfriend's arm was wrapped around her shoulder, and she was pressed against him, as if she wanted to disappear. Two girls sat together so absorbed in reading magazines that Katelyn decided they must be waiting for someone else who had already gone in to see the doctor.

Leah came and sat next to her, glancing at their companions. "Katelyn, I have to speak to the counselor first. Then I get prepped for surgery. After surgery, I have to wait a little while so they can keep an eye on me to be sure I can go home."

Katelyn nodded.

"They say you can stay with me except for the recovery room," Leah continued. "You can't come there because of protecting the other patients' privacy."

Katelyn looked at Leah, confused.

"Well, if you come in the recovery room, you'll know who had the procedure," she said.

"Yeah, I think I got that part," Katelyn said, still not sure whether Leah was asking her what she had guessed.

"Will you come with me then?"

Katelyn looked at her friend, her best friend. Just looking into her eyes, Katelyn could see how much Leah had changed since meeting Carter. "Yes," she said. "I will stay with you as long as you need me." She didn't want to. Nothing in her wanted to. She felt her stomach clench as she said the words. But it was Leah who was asking.

"Thanks," Leah said, then leaned back in her seat and closed her eyes. Her whole body relaxed.

The two girls sat without talking until Leah's name was called. They followed a nurse to a room that reminded Katelyn of a comfortable library. Sitting on a chair facing the couch sat a woman with a brilliant shock of white hair, dark brown eyes framed in wrinkles, and a warm, welcoming smile.

"Hi, I'm Elizabeth. And one of you is Leah Graham?"

Leah nodded, looking serious. Katelyn would have preferred talking to someone younger than her grandmother.

"Please sit," Elizabeth waved her hand at the couch.

Elizabeth asked Leah a number of medical questions, beginning with more general health conditions, then relating more specifically to Leah's menstrual periods and sexual behavior. She was polite, respectful, and direct. Leah answered everything in a similar manner. If she was embarrassed by any of the questions, she hid it well, Katelyn thought.

"Okay, here's what happens next," Elizabeth said. "We're going to do a pregnancy test to confirm you are pregnant. If the results are positive, do you want to terminate the pregnancy today?"

Leah nodded.

"You need to sign this consent form."

Leah took the pen offered her and signed her name boldly.

"I will give you a prescription for birth control for three months," Elizabeth said.

Katelyn was startled and looked at Leah, who also seemed surprised.

Elizabeth continued, "This will help your periods and hormones stabilize after the procedure today. If you want to continue to use the pill as your birth control, you just need to be aware that it will not offer protection against sexually transmitted diseases." She asked in a softer voice. "Have you thought about what method of birth control you'll use after this?"

"No," Leah said. "I haven't . . . I don't expect to have sex. I mean, I've only had one partner, and the relationship is over now."

Elizabeth's dark eyes were compassionate. "I understand. We . . ." she smiled. "Those of us who work at the clinic, I mean, prefer not to have repeat business. If you haven't thought that far, that's fine. You'll have three months to figure it out while you take this prescription." She handed it to Leah. "And, by that time, I hope you'll have a plan."

"I'm sure I won't need it after the three months," Leah said, shaking her head no as if to emphasize her point.

"Still, once you have had sex, it is much easier to have it again. I just want you to take precautions."

Leah's eyes blazed into Elizabeth's. "Sometimes the best of precautions are ruined by a man who is determined to trap a girl."

Elizabeth studied her for a moment before answering. "I hear you. It is an unfortunate way to have to grow up and lose one's innocence. But these experiences often make starry-eyed girls into strong women who know what they want."

Katelyn looked from one to the other, wondering if the counselor had gone too far. But then Leah nodded and gave the older woman a slim, begrudging smile. "Yes," she said, standing up and holding out her hand to shake Elizabeth's. "That's a good goal for me. Thank you."

CHAPTER 4

When the girls arrived at the Neufeld's house Monday after their trip to the clinic, Katelyn discovered two messages on the answering machine. She scowled. This complication had not occurred to her. She got Leah settled on the couch, tucked a blanket around her, and watched as her friend fell asleep almost instantly. Katelyn thought a quick desperate prayer for Leah's recovery and healing, then got up to find out who had called.

"Hi, Katelyn, it's me," Shawn said. "I assume you're not feeling well or you could be skipping school." He laughed. "Yeah, right. Anyway, I hope you feel better soon. I'll check in with you later. Thanks for a terrific day yesterday."

Then the beep and Katelyn's mom said, "I'm on my lunch break, dear. Just wanted to see how you were feeling. Please call me back when you hear this. I'm worried about you."

Katelyn called her mom back right away. "I must have been in the shower when you called," she lied. She didn't have to lie about her headache. It was worse. She went upstairs to take a couple of aspirin before joining Leah in the living room. She sat quietly, remembering how the doctor had been so gentle with her, telling her what to expect, when he would touch her, what might hurt a little. There was a moment when Leah caught her breath as if in pain. Then the procedure was over, and the nurse was removing the plastic bowl that held the embryo, whisking it out of the room before either Katelyn or Leah could glimpse its contents. Katelyn was relieved for their discretion.

Leah stirred briefly in her sleep, and Katelyn's eyes were drawn to her face, half hidden by her stunning black curls, now streaked with maroon highlights. She watched her friend for a long time, troubled by the bridge they had crossed together that day, wondering if they would ever find their way back to happier times.

By the time Rachel got back from dance class, all signs of Leah were gone, and Katelyn's headache had escalated. Rachel took one look at her sister stretched out on the couch and called Mom at work.

"Mom, Katelyn's so bad, you should come home," Rachel said. "She says the light hurts her eyes, and she feels like she's going to throw up. Plus, she's lying on the couch not doing anything."

Rachel listened for a minute, then said, "Okay, bye." She looked at Katelyn. "She's on her way home. She's going to call the doctor first and get that prescription he recommended the last time you saw him and he thought you had migraines."

"I've already taken aspirin . . ." Katelyn began.

"Which isn't helping. Is there anything I can do?"

"Just sit here with me."

"Okay, move," Rachel ordered. "Just sit up for a minute." Katelyn sat up and felt the room swirl around her head. Rachel slipped onto the couch and motioned for Katelyn to put her head down on her lap. After Katelyn lay down, Rachel gently massaged her head and neck. Katelyn felt the muscles relax, and she drifted in and out of sleep.

When Mom arrived, she gave Katelyn a small pill to take. "The doctor said you should start feeling some relief in about an hour. He also suggested a hot shower or bath."

Katelyn sat up slowly, feeling her head pound with each beat of her heart. Mom helped her stand up, slipping her arm around Katelyn's waist to steady her.

"I'll go run the water," Rachel said, leading the way.

An hour later, Katelyn was feeling much better. In her flannel pajamas and fleece robe, snuggled between her mother and her sister on the couch, Katelyn felt warm and loved and pain free. She felt a little guilty accepting all this pampering, as if she were the one who had gone through a medical procedure today instead of Leah. Just as she was wondering how Leah was doing, the telephone rang. Rachel jumped up to answer it.

When Rachel handed the phone to Katelyn, she remembered she had forgotten to call Shawn back.

But the male voice that answered her was not Shawn's. "Hey, Katelyn, it's Noah."

"Oh, hi," she said, standing up and moving toward her bedroom.

"Not too long, dear," Mom called to her. "I want you to go to bed early tonight."

"Okay," Katelyn answered. As soon as she was out of earshot, she said, "Have you talked to Leah?"

"Yes. Briefly. She sounded relieved. So, tell me, how did it go today?"

"I think it went well. No complications, if that's what you mean. She slept here afterwards, then ate a snack before going home."

"Tell me, Katelyn, did they treat her well? I need to know," Noah said.

Once she began to tell him, she found herself telling him everything, from the beginning to the end of the day, when she'd walked Leah out to her car and said goodbye. Noah listened to every detail, never interrupting her, but asking questions whenever she paused.

When Katelyn finished, they were both silent.

"And how are you?" Noah asked, breaking the silence.

"I've got a migraine, but the medicine's working so right now I don't have any pain."

"Have you had them before?" he asked, sounding concerned.

"Not this bad," she said. "This was the first time I felt like I was going to throw up."

"I'm sorry. Is there anything I can do for you, Katelyn?"

"No," she said, without stopping to think.

He laughed, but it sounded almost bitter.

It was Katelyn's turn to apologize. "I'm sorry. Noah, you are a good brother to Leah. You take good care of her. I . . . I find myself wishing there was someone like you in my life."

"There is someone like me in your life, Katelyn. Someone exactly like me, in fact."

"What?"

"Not what, who. I just meant, if you need someone to be like a big brother to you, I'm available." Noah's voice was warm. "You always come across so independent, Katelyn, but I'm sure this last year, with your parents separating and all, hasn't been easy for you."

She felt a pang go through her, and tears start in her eyes. "Thanks, Noah. Maybe. . . ." Maybe what? Maybe she could talk to him if he weren't so infuriating? Maybe she had misjudged him? Maybe loving Leah wasn't the only thing they had in common?

"Whatever. Katelyn, if you've got what you need to get by, I know you won't be calling me. But let me give you my number anyway, just in case you need to talk or in case anything happens with Leah that you think I'd want to know." Katelyn wrote the phone number down carefully, just in case. Then she tucked the slip of paper into the top drawer of her dresser and said goodbye.

Tuesday morning before their first class, Shawn was pacing the hall by Katelyn's locker. When he made her out in the crowd, his grin lit up his face. She smiled back, glad for the warm welcome. Then, almost as quickly, she realized she owed him an apology.

"Oh, Shawn, I'm sorry I didn't call you back," she said quickly. "I meant to, but then Noah called to check on Leah again and I forgot." A chill went through her. She had not meant to say as much as she had. She did not want to give away Leah's secret.

But Shawn didn't seem to think anything was odd. He slipped his arm around her, gave her a quick squeeze, then let go. "It's okay. So what happened yesterday?"

"I . . . woke up with a bad headache. But it's better today."

Shawn studied her, then nodded. "Glad you're better," he said, looking down.

"Meet you in the cafeteria for lunch?" Katelyn asked, grabbing the sleeve of Shawn's jacket before he walked away.

"Sure," he said. "Then maybe you can tell me the truth about yesterday." Before she could say another word, he turned and threaded his way through the sea of students.

Katelyn was left staring after him. What could he know about what she did yesterday? Or what did he think he knew?

The bell rang, and Katelyn moved mechanically toward her first class. She wasn't sure she could face Shawn without first talking to Leah. Maybe Leah would let her tell Shawn something that would be less of a lie.

After her second class, Katelyn made a run for the pay phone, hurriedly punching in the Grahams' number. On the third ring, Leah's voice sang out "hello" so cheerfully, Katelyn couldn't believe she had reached her friend.

"Leah?"

"This is Leah Graham. Who's this?"

"It's me, Katelyn, you idiot."

Leah laughed. "Well, I thought it was you, Katelyn, but then you're supposed to be at school, so that didn't make any sense. What's up?"

Katelyn heard a squeal in the background.

"Jonah wants to talk to you," Leah reported.

"Not now," Katelyn said. She didn't have time for Jonah right now.

"Not now," Leah told Jonah.

"Shawn and I are having lunch today."

"Well, that'll be nice."

Katelyn sighed. "Leah, he suspects something about yesterday. What should I tell him?"

"Yes, we're all sitting around the dining room

table studying geography with this new teaching game Mom bought last week—Mom, Joshua, and Jonah," Leah said.

"Can I tell Shawn where I was yesterday? I hate to lie to him."

"No. But you did help me with that paper so you should know the answer," Leah said.

Katelyn was quiet, frantically trying to decipher the meaning in her friend's words.

"So, I can tell him I was with you, and that you needed me, but not why?"

"Yes, I'd say that's right," Leah said. "Now next time, Katelyn, you need to spend more time reading the assigned material rather than checking the answers with your brilliant, home-schooled best friend."

"I'll remember that," Katelyn muttered, hanging up the phone.

At lunch, Katelyn and Shawn had sat down at the table before they spoke. She decided to wait for him to start.

Finally, he did. "I tried to call you a few times . . ."

"I got one message."

He nodded, then continued. "My third period got canceled, so I drove over to see if you were okay. I rang the doorbell a few times, but no one answered. So, I'm thinking you weren't home."

Katelyn tried to open her milk carton, but couldn't get it. Shawn took it from her, opened the other end of the cardboard fold, and set it back down on her tray. He was studying her.

"I was with Leah. I didn't ask my parents because I didn't think they'd let me stay home with her. And her parents don't know either."

"How is she?" he asked. "Leah."

"She's. . . ." Katelyn had started to say "fine," but realized it wasn't true. When she thought about Leah, she had mixed feelings. She was angry with Leah. And, yet, when she had watched Leah sleeping on her couch, she felt waves of tenderness for this young girl who had been through so much.

Shawn was still waiting for an answer.

"I don't know," Katelyn said. "I really don't know how she is. But you won't tell, right?"

"No," he said. "Not a word to anyone."

He sounded so sure, she wished he was the one keeping the secret, not her. She longed to lean over and tell him the whole truth, right then and there. She felt somehow it would help her to get it out of her system, as if her confession would strip the action of its power and allow the sin to be forgiven.

But she didn't say anything. She took a sip of her milk and a bite of her sloppy joe. It felt lumpy and tasteless in her mouth.

"It's okay, Katelyn. You're taking care of Leah."

"Let's talk about something else," she said, spitting out her food into her napkin.

That afternoon, when Katelyn found she couldn't concentrate on her schoolwork, she busied herself by straightening up her room, picking up piles of outfits she had worn the previous week and dumping them into her clothes basket. She took them downstairs to put a load of clothes in the washer, stopping long enough to empty the pockets of her jeans. She had a vague recollection of tucking something important into her pocket a few days ago. Then she remembered what she was looking for, the slip of paper Mrs. Hurley had scribbled her phone number on. She looked for the pants she had worn to Redbud, realizing wryly she needed only to have smelled them to identify them. She filled the washing machine, dumped in some laundry soap, and ran upstairs to dial the number.

Mrs. Hurley answered on the second ring, speaking quietly.

"Hi, it's Katelyn Neufeld from the Redbud Riders

program. I was wondering if it would be okay if I dropped by for a few minutes to see Kiana."

"Sure, Katelyn. That would mean a lot to her. She's napping now, but you can come any time."

"Is there anything I can bring? That she'd enjoy?"

"No, she's got everything she needs. She'll just be happy to see you."

Katelyn looked at the clock. It was four-thirty. Her mom wasn't home from work yet, and Rachel was at Hillary's. "How about I come now?" she suggested. "If you tell me how to get there, I could be there shortly."

Fifteen minutes later, Katelyn was standing outside the front door of a small two-story house with lots of windows. Before she could ring the bell, Mrs. Hurley pulled open the door.

"We're so glad you could come," she said, with a smile. She took Katelyn's coat, and motioned her into the living room where Kiana, eyes closed, was lying on the couch, a bright yellow afghan tucked up under her armpits. She looked like she had fallen asleep while drawing. Across her lap was a sketch pad. In her right hand was a short pencil, a stub worn down by her efforts. Drawings were strewn all over the coffee table, the floor, the easy chair closest to Kiana. Katelyn moved the only empty seat, a straight-backed wooden chair, so she could face the sleeping child.

"Hey baby," Mrs. Hurley called gently, coming into the living room with a small plate of cookies and two glasses of milk. "Wake up. You have company."

Kiana opened her eyes almost immediately. "Katie," she said, her voice hoarse, but her eyes bright with joy.

"Hi, Kiana. Nice to hear your voice again," Katelyn said, smiling. "Will you show me your drawings?"

The girl nodded, but closed her sketch pad and slid it to the floor. "Cookies first," she said as she pulled herself into a sitting position and looked at her mother, who balanced the tray on Kiana's lap. Mrs. Hurley straightened all the drawings into one pile, then took the glasses of milk from Kiana and set them on the table. She turned to leave, but Kiana stopped her.

"Mama?"

"It's all right, baby. I'm just going into the kitchen to wash some dishes and start supper. You enjoy your time with your friend. I'll be back before Katelyn leaves."

This seemed to satisfy Kiana, who relaxed against

the arm of the sofa and offered the cookies to Katelyn.

"What kind are they?" Katelyn asked. The cookie she held was homemade, dark brown, soft, and smelled like ginger and cinnamon.

"Molasses," Kiana said. "Mama makes them special for me."

"Well, thank you for sharing them with me."

Kiana smiled through the cookie in her mouth, and Katelyn wondered how much more frequently the girl used her facial expressions to communicate so she could save her voice.

But she didn't have much time to wonder. Kiana, after taking two bites from her cookie, set it down on the plate and patted the couch. "Pictures now," she said, dropping her feet slowly onto the floor and sitting so her back rested against the back of the couch. But she wasn't yet satisfied, and Katelyn noticed that as Kiana kept trying to get comfortable, she was becoming winded. Finally, Kiana was where she wanted to be.

"Sit here," she said, patting the seat to her right. Katelyn sat down gently, and Kiana leaned against her.

"These?" Katelyn gestured at the pile of drawings

on the coffee table. "Or the sketchpad?" she asked, reaching for the pad alongside the couch.

"Yes," Kiana nodded.

Katelyn put the drawings on top of the sketch pad. The drawings were colorful and dramatic, a child's pictures of her mother, a hospital monitor, yellow ducklings on a violet pond, Trim Jim and the other Redbud horses, other children, the night sky. Some were begun in pencil, then completed in colored pencils or crayons or even watercolors. Katelyn tried to say something different about each one. "The duck looks like she's about to fly off the water. Trim Jim looks happy to see you. Your mother looks tired in this one. Who's this with the red hair?"

Kiana giggled then, tugging quickly on a handful of Katelyn's hair.

Katelyn looked more carefully at the picture. Yes, it was her, in Trim Jim's stable, with a tiny Kiana sitting on a hay bale waiting. Kiana had drawn Katelyn with her hand holding onto Trim Jim's mane, as if she was preparing to mount him. On the other side of the stall, the face of a young man watched her, a boy with blond hair and one large card in his hand, a card with a small fish drawn on it.

"Well, look at this. You've drawn Shawn as well," Katelyn said, amazed. A few months earlier, Katelyn and Shawn had visited Kiana in the hospital. Shawn had played the card game "Go Fish" with Kiana.

Kiana nodded, excited. "My life. My friends. My pictures," she said.

Suddenly Katelyn understood. "You've drawn the pictures for the book your mother is writing about you. Is that right, Kiana?"

"Yes, yes, Katie."

"But why are we in the stable?"

"You and Trim Jim go together."

Katelyn nodded. That made sense. And Shawn was associated with Katelyn. But the cards were from being in the hospital.

"And he," Kiana pointed at the boy's face, "felt like Redbud."

Katelyn nodded, fighting back tears. She squeezed Kiana's shoulder. "Yes, he makes me feel I'm in a happier place, too."

Driving home after her visit with Kiana, Katelyn found herself thinking about what it must be like to live so close to death all the time. She felt she took her health and her life for granted, and that somehow, this lack of gratitude was a shameful thing. If she could learn how to be grateful for every moment, to really live each day to the fullest and to appreciate it, it would somehow honor her friendship with

Kiana. Not that it would make the girl healthy and strong, but it would somehow make her a better person, more worthy of Kiana's affection.

When she arrived home, Katelyn found Rachel sitting in the living room, immersed in a science fiction novel.

"Mom's not home yet?" Katelyn asked, disappointed.

Rachel shook her head no, then looked up from her book. "She called and said she'd be home around six-thirty. Oh, and Leah called and asked you to call her back."

"Rachel, how about we surprise Mom and make supper?"

Her face lit up. "Yeah, let's. We've got what, almost a half hour before she's home?"

"Something like that."

"There's hamburger in the fridge. If you want to fry them up, I'll make some jello."

Katelyn laughed. "Great, I get the raw meat, and you get the fun part."

"Well, it was your idea. You can make the jello if you want. It's just that I know you can season the hamburgers better than I can." Rachel stood up and made her way to the kitchen.

"Is that a real compliment or a bribe?" Katelyn asked.

"Let's say it was a compliment," Rachel said, giggling. Both girls hated handling raw meat, so Mom had learned not to count on them for help in that department.

Rachel went to the fridge and started unloading the hamburger, a tomato, a jar of pickles, a head of lettuce, mustard, and ketchup. "Do we have any buns?" she asked, opening the freezer compartment.

"If we don't, we can just use sliced bread or bagels."

"Yeah, bagels sound good. There are some new whole-wheat, billion-grain ones Mom got from the health food store. Let's try those."

The two girls worked together happily in the kitchen, cooking, slicing, finding a variety of foods to set on the table. When their mom arrived home, exactly at six-thirty, the table was set and Katelyn was just taking the hamburgers out of the frying pan.

"Girls, I'm so sorry I couldn't get here before now," Mom started, as she walked into the house. But then she saw the dining room table, and her face lit up.

Rachel grinned at her.

"You two are . . ." she started, then stopped.

"The cat's meow, the lights of your life, the best daughters ever?" Rachel asked.

Mom nodded.

"You are so blessed to have us," Katelyn added, holding the frying pan in one hand and the spatula in the other.

"I certainly am," Mom said, smiling warmly. "I had a rough day today. I struggled and struggled over the same problems until finally I had to ask my boss for help. Then once she explained it to me, I could see where I was getting stuck. But by then it was late, and I felt bad keeping you girls waiting for dinner. And, then I come home, and you've made dinner for me! You're getting so responsible and thoughtful, I am so proud of you."

"It was Katelyn's idea," Rachel said. "We had fun."

"Rachel had fun. She got to make the jello. I got to handle the raw meat," Katelyn said, grimacing at her sister.

But Rachel looked happy, happier than Katelyn had seen her in a long time. She knew this small project had touched her sister. She felt a pang go through her, as she realized Rachel still needed her. It was not long before Katelyn would be leaving home; she would need to be careful not to leave Rachel, too.

CHAPTER 5

Leah called Katelyn every day, wanting to talk, chatting away about small things, and keeping her on the phone long after Katelyn wanted to hang up. If Leah wanted to see her, she didn't ask, but rather gave small gentle hints, hoping Katelyn would offer. Finally, Saturday morning Leah called again.

"Hey Katelyn, I found a new kind of peanut butter and chocolate sandwich cookie to share with you. I even ordered them online," she said. Katelyn could hear the hope in her voice. Leah loved to eat cookies when the girls played chess, preferably sandwich cookies that had to be pried apart. Once Katelyn had pointed out this made the plastic chess players sticky with cookie crumbs, Leah had scooped them up and washed them in the bathroom sink.

Katelyn didn't answer at first. She was torn between being touched by the effort Leah had made and not wanting to see her yet.

"I haven't even opened them yet. I'm saving them for the next time you come over," Leah said, her voice almost pleading.

"Okay," Katelyn said. "How about I come over this afternoon, and we can play a few games of chess?"

"That would be great!" Leah said, with enthusiasm.

Katelyn hung up the phone. Leah had been through a lot these last few months. She doesn't deserve to lose her best friend on top of everything else, she told herself.

When she got to the Grahams, Katelyn found herself face to face with a completely different Leah than the one she had seen only five days earlier. Leah looked like she had stepped back in time to the girl she was before Carter. The dark circles under her eyes had eased somewhat, and there was a sparkle to her that Katelyn had missed.

Before they could say a word to each other, one of the twins came running down the stairs.

"Hey, Katelyn, what's up?" Jonah said.

She grinned at him. "Hey yourself, Jonah."

"I hear you got a new boyfriend."

"You heard that?" Katelyn looked at him in disbelief.

"Leah told me."

Leah gave him a playful shove. "And, you won't get any more information from me either if you can't keep your mouth shut about the source."

Jonah continued, "I asked her if you had time to help me with my homework now that Nathan was out of town, and she said you'd already found someone else. I was heartbroken, Katelyn. Here I've been waiting for you since I was four, and you don't even . . ."

She laughed. "Yeah, yeah, Jonah. We've been over this. Sorry, you missed your window of opportunity. You get your driver's license, then we'll talk." She started up the stairs, saying to Leah, "C'mon. Let's go play chess. Your brother's such a sweet talker, he almost made me forget why I'd come."

"He has that effect on people," Leah said, following her.

"Later, Kate," Jonah said.

"Yeah, much later," she said, but there was affection in her voice.

When they reached her room, Leah plopped down on her bed, grabbing one white pawn and one black in each hand and scrambling them behind her back. Katelyn chose the right hand, with the black pawn.

They played two games of chess, munching on the new cookies and barely talking. Katelyn won both games, which surprised her since she found it difficult to concentrate. She wondered if Leah was letting her win. Then Leah asked, "What's new with Shawn?"

"I think we're going steady."

Leah grinned at her. "About time. No, seriously, I'm glad. He's a good guy."

"Thanks." Katelyn felt awkward. "I was thinking that about Noah the last time I talked to him."

"Noah?! My brother Noah? No way!" Leah could not contain her amazement.

"Shut up." Katelyn could feel her face turning red.

"Okay, so I overreacted. Tell me," Leah said.

"He's just so concerned about you. I'm envious."

"Yeah, he's the best brother. He and Jenna broke up, and it's got to be killing him. But he sends me jokes in his letters to cheer me up and tells me funny stories about food fights."

"He and Jenna broke up?" Katelyn was surprised.

"Yeah. He's looking into transferring to a school closer to home for next fall. He'd only agreed to California for Jenna, if you remember." Leah had always been polite to Jenna, but Katelyn had sensed she didn't like her much, especially after Noah had followed her across the country.

"But . . . how can they get back together again, if he's here?" Katelyn couldn't help the frown that had creased her forehead.

"I guess they can't. I suspect that when they broke up, they weren't planning that part," Leah said, trying not to grin at her.

"It's not funny!" Katelyn found Leah's attempt at humor irritating and in poor taste.

Leah leaned back, studying her. "No, you're right. It's not funny. But you're acting as if this has something to do with you."

Katelyn was uneasy. "I just can't believe it, that's all. They always seemed like the perfect couple."

"I could have said that about you and Nathan. You could have said that about your parents."

"I gotta go," Katelyn said, standing up.

"Wait, wait, Katie. Don't go. I'm sorry."

But Katelyn had turned and was practically running out of Leah's room. Her parents' divorce, Noah and Jenna's breakup, her and Nathan's breakup, Leah's abortion—suddenly it was all too much. Everything seemed so unfair. Didn't anything last? Wasn't anything as good as it appeared? Was there always a dark side?

She drove around at first, not wanting to go home. Mom was home, but right now, the divorce seemed all her fault. Finally, Katelyn found herself downtown, so she drove to the island park. Her church had picnics there occasionally. She even remembered a few times when her family had gathered there. Katelyn loved the park, a small island that had formed between the city's two rivers. Three small bridges enabled pedestrians and bicyclists to enter the park, but no motor vehicles were allowed. Walking the trail around the outside perimeter of the island took less than ten minutes. But today, she settled into a playground swing and kicked herself back and forth while the tears of rage and sadness came.

Katelyn's shoes became encrusted with mud from the half-melted snow, but she didn't care. When the gray sky that had been threatening rain all day opened up and poured down on her, she still sat preoccupied by her thoughts of loss and despair. Finally, her thoughts cleared, and she stood up. She knew where she had to go and what to say. All the losses were gone, and there was only one. One loss that needed repair. Katelyn walked to her car, her sneakers squishing water like sponges being squeezed and refilled. She drove straight home, walked up the front steps, and opened the front door. She barely registered that the car in the driveway was Max's. She didn't care who was here. It mattered only that her mother was home, only that Katelyn could say the words she believed would mean enough to her mother that she would change the course of her life, of all their lives, so that magically, everything would return to the way it was.

When the door opened and Katelyn stepped into the room, Mom, Max, and Rachel turned toward her, the expressions in their eyes turning from curiosity to concern—as if they all felt the same thing, Katelyn would think later.

"Mom?" Katelyn's voice came out pleading and broken while tears streamed down her face. Mom was already on her feet, on her way to her oldest daughter. She stopped in front of her while Katelyn struggled to speak.

"Mom," she tried again, but it was too hard.

"Tell me, honey. What is it?"

"Please d-don't d-divorce D-d-daddy," Katelyn couldn't stop her teeth from chattering. "Please Mom." In her eyes, she tried to show her that the world would never be the same, that already things were spinning out of control. If her mother would reconsider, would step backwards, the world would be restored to its proper order.

Mom wrapped her warm arms around Katelyn. "Oh sweet girl. Oh, baby. Momma's got you," she crooned in her ear. The words echoed to Katelyn from years earlier, when she was a much smaller form pressed against her mother's larger, more powerful body. Here and now, with her mother holding her, it was disturbing to realize that she was taller than her mother, yet still her mother sang out the soothing, but powerless refrain. Katelyn's tears became wails as she realized she couldn't save her parents' marriage. She couldn't save anything or anyone.

Long before Katelyn was ready to let go of her mother, Rachel and Max were tugging at her to get warmed up. Rachel had run a bath for her, and she took Katelyn upstairs, starting to help her out of her clothes.

"I can do it," Katelyn said.

Rachel retreated, dropping the lid to the toilet and sitting down with her back to her sister.

Katelyn finished undressing, then climbed into the tub, pulling her knees up to her chin, tears streaming down her face, rocking back and forth.

"So what happened?" Rachel asked. "You went to Leah's, right?"

"Yeah."

"Did she beat you at chess?" Rachel asked.

"Good one," Katelyn sniffed. "No. But I think she let me win."

Rachel waited.

Katelyn sank down into the water.

Then she said, "Noah and Jenna broke up."

"I see. So now, but for Shawn, you could go after the love of your life?" Rachel baited her, using the absurd to get to the truth.

"Yeah, right," Katelyn said. "But you're not surprised."

"No. It always bugged me how Jenna asked for everything, and Noah gave her everything and more."

Katelyn didn't understand. "But she's the one leaving him."

"Exactly. Why would he leave her? He's been giving his life blood to get her to like him. What if he had stopped?"

"But he adored her!" Katelyn could not quite wrap her mind around this new view of Noah and Jenna's relationship.

"Of course. As long as she's the center of the universe, they have the perfect formula."

"Maybe you're right. But if he was giving her everything, why would she leave him?"

Rachel shrugged. "Maybe she got tired of it. Maybe she wanted something more than her own personal Santa Claus."

A silence fell over the room.

Rachel cleared her throat as if to speak, but Katelyn beat her to it. "So, what do you think Mom and Dad got tired of?"

"Each other."

Katelyn shook her head and snorted. She reached for a towel and stood up. Maybe it was all just that simple.

For the rest of the evening, Rachel barely left Katelyn's side. When Katelyn got quiet, Rachel would reach out to her, telling her a story, showing her something, encouraging her to play cribbage, or making cupcakes. When the phone rang, Rachel told first Shawn, then Leah that Katelyn wasn't feeling well, but she would call them back the next day.

Mom and Max watched over her, too, taking their cues from Rachel, who seemed to know instinctively how to keep her just occupied enough that her thoughts couldn't take her back into the place she knew was irrational, the place where she really had believed everything could be set right again, if only her parents could be together.

When Katelyn went to bed, Mom followed her in to say goodnight.

"I know it's hard," Mom began.

"No. You don't." Katelyn looked at her, pleading. "I'm not talking back, Mom. But you really have no idea at all how hard it is. Not just you and Dad, but everything else that's going on right now."

"Tell me, Katelyn. What else is going on right now?"

She shrugged and looked away.

"So, if you can't talk to me, would you like to talk to someone else?"

"No," Katelyn said. What was the point? She couldn't talk about Leah, about how angry she was with her. She couldn't talk about how she had failed to make Leah change her mind. She couldn't talk about how different the world seemed, with relationships ending that she had always believed in. Everything was tangled up with everything else. She didn't know how to sort out the strands, to separate them into distinct events.

"I was thinking of a counselor, or a pastor, or even an older friend?" Mom continued. "It would be someone who would keep it confidential. You could say whatever you need to and know it would stop there."

Katelyn rubbed her eyes. "No," she said again. If she started talking, she wasn't sure she could stop.

"You don't have to decide tonight," Mom said. "Just think about it."

"Okay," Katelyn said. No, she thought. She couldn't do it. What was the point in talking about it? Nothing would change. Things wouldn't go back to the way they were.

Almost as soon as Mom had left the room, Rachel slipped in, whispering, "Hey, Katelyn."

"Hey Rachel. How's my favorite nursemaid? Is it time for my enema yet?"

Rachel giggled. "You're bad." She crossed the room and crawled into bed with Katelyn, taking her hand and squeezing it. "Can I sleep in here with you tonight?"

"I guess. As long as you don't hog the covers," Katelyn said, yawning as she moved over to make room. The girls were quiet. Katelyn heard Rachel's breath slow, felt her body twitch, and within moments, both girls were sound asleep.

Sunday morning, Katelyn woke early, feeling completely rested and oddly enough, cheerful. She could hear the rain and the wind blowing against her window. But she felt warm and safe inside. She crawled carefully out of bed to avoid waking Rachel and made her way to the kitchen.

She started brewing a pot of coffee, then decided to make blueberry muffins while she was waiting for the others to get up. She rustled through the kitchen for the ingredients she needed, enjoying the quiet.

It was only six-thirty when Katelyn pulled the muffins out of the oven and dumped them on some paper towels to cool. By now, she was impatient for everyone else to get up so she'd have someone to talk to, but it would likely be another half hour before Mom got up. It was too early to return either Shawn's or Leah's phone calls. In fact, the only person Katelyn could count on being up this early was her father, she realized, grinning as the idea hit her. Dad was up by five every day—writing, grading papers, doing research, or preparing for class.

He answered on the fourth ring, sounding distracted.

"Trouble finding the phone again, Dad?" Katelyn asked, trying not to laugh as she imagined him sorting through the mess on his desk for the telephone.

He grunted. "Well, you know me. It's got to be somewhere between the pages of an anatomy textbook or filed with the molecular slides of a species of elm trees."

"Too true."

"So what's gotten into you that you're awake so early? Are you considering following your father into academic life?"

"Not really. It still seems a little early for me to decide on a career path—not early in the morning, but early in my life."

"I knew I wanted to be a professor when I was 12."

"Yes, when the miracle of life was revealed to you." Katelyn loved the image of her father as a tall, skinny redhead with a crew cut catching tadpoles on the pond at his uncle's farm in southern Manitoba, then tending them carefully in an old bathtub in his backyard, watching fascinated as they were magically transformed from fish-like beings into the frogs they were meant to be.

"We're all growing and changing every moment. All of life is moving towards its destiny—whether the changes are visible or not. You and I are moving toward our destinies."

Katelyn was quiet for a moment, wondering how to tell him what she had been thinking about the day before. How it was not beginnings that occupied her thoughts, but endings. "So, Dad, you're okay then?"

"Yes. I'm starting to get a little hungry for breakfast, but that's normal for this time of day."

"Putting aside your biological needs for the moment, Dad. I mean, are you doing okay about the divorce?"

"Hmm."

Katelyn did not find this answer helpful. "I mean, if Mom were willing to work things out, Dad, would you too?"

He was quiet.

"Well, Dad?"

"I don't know, Katelyn, to be honest. But I assume if your mother did want to work things out, she would be calling me." His words were gentle, but she felt he was telling her to butt out.

"Obviously, though, you would like us to work things out," he continued. "And, that's what we should be talking about, honey. Your feelings."

"I want you to be together."

Dad sighed. "Yes, I know. That is what you've known all your life. It's natural for you to want it back. But, my darling daughter, your mother and I have agreed that the divorce is necessary. Our living together had become quite painful for both of us. That doesn't mean it is right for us to make you and Rachel unhappy. We are both terribly sorry for the pain this is causing the two of you. Still, I think we are all seeing your mother happier these last few months than she has been in years."

"And what about you, Dad? Are you happy too?"

He spoke slowly. "I am at peace, Katelyn. I believe better times are coming, for all of us. And, I hope that someday I'll meet someone and, you know, fall in love again."

"Sometimes . . ." Katelyn choked. "Sometimes, Dad, you seem so . . . lonely."

"And, so you worry about me? Feel sorry for me?"

"Yes, I guess so."

"Then we—your mother and I—have done a good job of teaching you empathy, Katelyn. This is good that you can put yourself in other people's shoes and imagine their feelings. But it is also a lie. Because it is your feelings you're giving them, not theirs. I am rarely lonely because I have my work. My work gives my life a meaning and purpose I have never been able to find in a relationship, except perhaps in my relationships with you and Rachel."

Katelyn recognized the truth in her father's words. His work was his life, and, as such, it insulated him from the loss of his home life. He, out of all of them, had probably lost the least. Mom had lost her role as wife and stay-at-home mother. But she had also gained a new sense of herself and her capabilities by going back to work, as well as a new joy from her relationship with Max. Katelyn had lost the home she'd known, but it was a home she was already leaving as she felt herself pulled to her own place in the world, the destiny her father said she was moving toward. Rachel had lost the most—everyone was moving away from her, and she still needed them. These were the thoughts Katelyn was having as she said goodbye to her father, grabbed a couple of muffins, and went to wake up her sister.

CHAPTER 6

Katelyn kept busy the following week, trying to catch up on her homework. No matter how hard she tried to concentrate, everything took her twice as long to complete. She arranged her time, planning out her days so she wouldn't have a spare moment. She called Leah back early in the week and apologized for running out on her, but stopped short of suggesting they get together again.

"It was my fault," Leah said. "I should have known you're still dealing with your parents' divorce.

You can talk to me about it, you know. I want to be there for you."

Katelyn shook her head. "It's not that easy, Leah. It's not words. It's just feelings—a lot of feelings."

"I can still listen, Katelyn. You know I'm here for you. You can come over anytime."

"Not now," she said.

On Saturday, Katelyn arrived at Redbud only to discover that many of the children were out sick. She cleaned stalls and did odd jobs as instructed through the first class, worrying about Kiana. Just before the second class, Natalie, the director, stopped by to tell her and Pat that Chad, the boy who rode after Kiana, was running late so they should get his horse, Old Hoss, ready and meet him in the ring.

"Any word on Kiana?" Katelyn asked, heaving the saddle across Old Hoss.

Natalie nodded. "Yes. I meant to tell you. She's resting at home. Mrs. Hurley thinks she is feeling a little better, but a new medication just makes her so tired she doesn't have the energy for class."

"Well, at least she's not in the hospital," Pat said.

"Yeah, it always feels better to know our kids are at home, doesn't it?" Natalie said, turning to go.

Katelyn smiled in agreement as she tightened the girth around the horse's belly.

Pat lead Old Hoss out to the ring, while Katelyn walked beside them.

"You're very fond of her, aren't you?" Pat asked, turning slightly so Katelyn could hear her.

"Who?"

"Kiana."

"Yes, I am." Katelyn smiled, remembering the drawings Kiana had shared with her when she had visited her.

Pat stopped in the ring and turned to look directly at her. "Be careful," she said. "These children . . . they'll break your heart if you let them."

Katelyn stared at her, shocked. Pat, who had worked at Redbud for longer than ten years, was warning her. Katelyn had observed Pat to be quiet with the children, but warm. Was she afraid of loving them?

Before Katelyn could think of an answer, Chad loped up to them and swung himself up onto Old Hoss.

"Hey, hey, Kate. Hey, hey, Pat. Hey, Old Hoss," Chad said, looking down at them.

"Hey Chad, how are you?" Katelyn asked.

"Doing fine. Very fine today. Had a great week. Love this rain. The plants always need the rain, right? Farmers always like rain, right?" Chad was looking at Pat when he said this since he remembered her brothers were farmers.

"That's right," Pat said, smiling. "My brothers were very happy with all the rain."

Chad beamed, glad to be right.

For the rest of the lesson, Katelyn found herself watching Pat with Chad, assessing whether the woman was holding back. But Pat seemed to be having fun, telling Chad knock-knock jokes she'd learned from her six-year-old nephew. If she was being "careful" as she'd advised Katelyn to do, it didn't show.

Back at home, when Katelyn opened the front door, Rachel jumped up to greet her.

"Shawn and Jason called a few minutes ago," she began. The four had been planning to go bowling later that afternoon. Bowling was a favorite pastime of the Roberts' family. Katelyn had gone once with Shawn, and Jason had been wanting to take Rachel.

"And?" Katelyn prompted.

Rachel's eyes were shining. "So, they wondered how we'd feel about inviting all the parents. They said their folks were free and open to coming if we liked the idea and suggested we invite Mom and Max."

Katelyn laughed, then plopped down in an armchair. "Sort of like a quadruple date?"

"Or a double-double date."

"What did you tell them?" Katelyn wanted to say yes, she thought it would be fun. But when Rachel had said they'd wanted to invite "all the parents," she had immediately thought of her dad. He'd be sitting home alone, working. Not that he would necessarily mind, or even know he hadn't been invited. But she wasn't sure she was ready for her mom to be part of a new couple, even if part of that couple was a man who seemed as friendly as Max.

"I told them my vote was yes, but I'd wait and ask you."

"What about Dad?"

"You know, I did think about Dad," Rachel said. "But then I realized we were talking bowling, not a trip to a library or museum." She laughed. "Even if he came, you know, he's such a klutz. I don't think he'd enjoy it much."

Katelyn nodded, feeling better. "Yeah, I guess you're right. Bowling's not his thing."

"I'll call them back and tell them it's okay. I already invited Mom and Max, on the condition you said it was fine. She and Max are thrilled to be asked."

Katelyn gave her a disbelieving look.

"Well, Max is excited about it, and he's trying to convince her it will be fun."

"That's a little more believable. But Rach . . . ?"

"Yeah?"

"Next time, let's invite Dad." Katelyn was thinking her mom had Max to do fun things with, and her Dad had only the two of them. She didn't want to make a habit of leaving him out.

"I thought of that already," Rachel said, holding up a page from the newspaper and pointing at it. "You know how Dad taught us to play chess? Well, there's a chess club that meets Thursday nights, and I'm going to see if Dad will go with me. You could come, too. And, maybe Leah would be interested as well."

Katelyn nodded and went upstairs to get ready for bowling. It was a great idea for Rachel to play chess with Dad. And, she might even like to join them occasionally. She knew Leah would love the idea. But she couldn't imagine herself inviting Leah right now. Maybe later.

Before Katelyn had finished dressing, she heard the doorbell ring, and Rachel called for her to hurry up. She tucked her shirt in, pulled on her socks, and slipped into her loafers as quickly as she could.

Downstairs she found Shawn and Jason standing in the living room, talking to Rachel.

"Mom and Max are meeting us there," Rachel said, turning to her.

Katelyn nodded. "And the Roberts?"

Shawn grinned. "They're waiting for us in the car. We'll all be jammed in. I hope you don't mind. They did say we could ditch them later and go out for shakes on our own."

"Like they're such a burden," Rachel said, rolling her eyes.

"They can be," Jason said, laughing at her.

"But not when they're bowling," Shawn added, taking Katelyn's coat from her and holding it for her to slip her arms in. He squeezed her shoulders before putting his hand on her back to hurry her out the door. Then he followed her out, with Jason next, and Rachel locking the door behind them.

The bowling alley was teeming with people. Katelyn felt her breath catch and a shiver go through her. The last time she had been around this many people packed in such a small space was at Rachel's dance recital when Carter had attacked Leah. But neither Leah nor Carter were here now, so why was she so tense, she wondered.

"C'mon," Shawn's father took charge. "Shawn,

take the girls to get their shoes. I see a free table over in the corner. Jason, go grab it. I'll find out how long before we can get a lane."

Shawn shifted his bowling ball to his other hand and reached for Katelyn's hand. He pulled her through the crowd, to the counter with the shoes. Rachel followed. Once the girls had gotten their shoes, they joined Jason at the table, lining up in a row of four. Mrs. Roberts, Shawn's mom, arrived a few minutes later carrying a pitcher of root beer. Mr. Roberts carried plastic cups and a bowl of popcorn.

"So, now we wait," he said.

"And, get to know each other a bit," Mrs. Roberts added, smiling broadly.

"Too bad we didn't bring the cribbage board," Jason said, sounding nervous.

"We'd need two," Rachel said.

"So what's the status report on the lanes?" Shawn asked.

"He thought we'd have a couple of lanes in a half hour. Not too bad," his dad said.

"So how are things at the shelter, Mrs. Roberts?" Katelyn asked.

She smiled. "Very well, thank you. We just had a successful food drive, so we're well stocked to meet our clients' needs. Of course, you and your sister are always welcome to come down and help us out. It was so sweet of you both to come on Thanksgiving."

Rachel grinned at her, then at Jason. Katelyn could see her sister reach for Jason's hand under the table.

"We're the perfect dates," Rachel said, giggling. "Make a good impression on the parents and the guys at the same time."

First Shawn and Katelyn burst out laughing, then his parents joined in.

"And, how is your friend . . . Leah?" Mrs. Roberts asked Katelyn.

She hesitated, uncertain how to answer.

"Leah calls Katelyn nearly every day," Rachel volunteered, casting a meaningful glance at her sister. Jason shifted uneasily in his chair and whispered, "She asked Katelyn, not you."

"As if she'd know," Rachel whispered back, loud enough for Katelyn to hear.

"I think she'll be okay, with time," Katelyn said, keeping her eyes on Shawn's mom and ignoring Rachel and Jason, who were still whispering, but more quietly now.

"And it's great she has your friendship," Mrs. Roberts said.

"That's exactly what I keep telling her," Rachel

jumped in, glaring defiantly at Katelyn, who was so surprised, she spilled her bowl of popcorn.

Just then, Shawn stood up and called out, "Mrs. Neufeld. Max, we're over here."

Jason asked, "Why did you call him by his first name?"

"I don't know his last name." He looked at Katelyn, who shook her head. She didn't know Max's last name either.

But Mrs. Roberts' hospitality took over, and she held out her hand to the two newcomers. "Hi, I'm Viv Roberts, and this is my husband Jim."

"Liz Neufeld, and this is my friend Max Bauman," Mom said, shaking Mrs. Roberts' hand.

Katelyn, Jason, and Shawn glanced at each other. Then Jason said, his voice lilting, "Mr. Bauman, sir, we're so glad you and your guest could join us tonight." Rachel's eyes widened in surprise.

Max chuckled and addressed the adults. "If it's okay with you, I'd rather the kids just call me Max."

Mr. Roberts nodded. "Sure. Have a seat and help yourself to the food. We should be getting our lanes in a few minutes."

Shortly after Mom and Max arrived, an announcement directed the Roberts' party to Lanes 1 and 2. Katelyn was glad they were at one end of the bowling alley, relieved not to have people on both sides of them. She had gotten comfortable in the corner. Now, as they walked back, she reached for Shawn's hand, grabbing it like a scared child on a busy city street. He glanced at her face, then squeezed her hand.

"What's wrong?" he asked, leaning toward her when they reached their lanes.

"Being around all these people reminds me of . . ." her voice trailed off, but she rubbed the scar on her arm where Carter's knife had caught and torn her skin.

Shawn studied her. The others had joined them by then. Rachel and Jason had already begun typing their names into the keyboard, pitting the adults against each other. Shawn leaned down and spoke into Jason's ear, then took Katelyn's hand and walked her out of the bowling alley toward the parking lot.

As soon as they were outside and away from the entrance, he kissed her softly on the cheek. Then he put his arms around her and held her for a few long moments, gently moving his hands up and down her back until she began to relax.

"Tell me," he said, wrapping an arm around her and starting to walk with her around the edge of the parking lot.

But Katelyn wasn't sure she understood it herself. "I was just scared all of the sudden."

Shawn nodded. "They're just people in there."

She didn't answer.

He tried again. "They're just like you and me. They love and they hate. They do good things and bad things. But most of us do them for a reason, Katelyn. Even Carter did what he did for a reason." He stopped and looked at her.

Yes, Katelyn knew that. Although she didn't like what Carter had done, she could see there was an odd sort of reason to it. "Yeah. You're right."

"No one in there wants to hurt you," Shawn said. "They're just loud. They're just having fun and being rowdy."

Katelyn nodded. Still, she felt her fear just beneath the surface. She wondered how Leah could leave her house, how she faced the fear of running into Carter again. She took a deep breath to clear her head and reached again for Shawn's hand. "I'm ready. Let's go face our competition."

The bowling party turned out to be a great success. Katelyn and Shawn waited for Jason and Rachel to finish their game, then played one foursome. Then Katelyn and Shawn moved over to play Mom and Max. Katelyn was impressed to see that Max, although he was soundly beaten by Shawn, was a pretty good bowler in his own right. Each game they tried to pair up the various players differently to keep things interesting. Once the mothers played against the daughters, and the men against the sons. The Roberts family was clearly the best, but they were such gracious winners that everyone had fun.

On the drive back to the Neufelds, Shawn stopped and picked up two milkshakes—one for him and Katelyn and the other for Jason and Rachel to share. The four of them played a couple of games of cribbage, then Katelyn and Shawn drifted off into the living room where they sat and talked about nothing in particular.

Afterwards, as Katelyn was climbing into bed, she reflected on how much fun they'd all had together and how comfortable she was with Shawn. Then she remembered something. She padded back down the stairs toward the kitchen. The lights were out, except for the lamp in the dining room. Rachel had gone to bed. Only their mother was still up. As she passed through the living room, Katelyn could hear her mother's voice, as soft as the lighting. But she couldn't hear what her mother was saying until she was almost upon her. Then, just a split second before Katelyn rounded the corner and met her mother's eyes, she heard her say, "I love you, Max." She felt like the wind had been knocked out of her. When had she last heard her mother tell her father she loved him?

"I . . . I gotta go, Max, dear," Mom said, her voice suddenly too loud in the darkened room. "I'll call you tomorrow. Katelyn's up and needs something." She hung up and spoke in a quieter, more matter-of-fact voice. "Is there something you needed, Katelyn?"

"I . . . was just going to use the phone," Katelyn stammered, trying to remember who she was going to call.

"Well, it's free now." Mom stood up. "I'm going to bed."

Katelyn wanted to say something about what she had heard, wanted her mother to acknowledge that this moment of profound intimacy had been interrupted, but Mom seemed intent on pretending nothing was wrong. She knew she would have been embarrassed if Mom had overheard her telling Shawn she loved him. Why was her mother acting like this?

Mom brushed by her, then turned back. "Thanks, again, Katelyn, for inviting me and Max to go bowling. We had a terrific time. And, it was fun to get to know all of the Roberts. They seem like such . . . good people."

Katelyn nodded and tried to smile. "Yes, Mom. You're welcome. We had a good time, too."

Once Mom was upstairs, Katelyn sat in the kitchen for a few long moments. If her mother already loved Max, was it possible that she would marry him? Then Max would be her and Rachel's stepfather? She felt uneasy. She didn't want things to change again. She hadn't gotten used to her parents' separation. It was too soon for her to think of them with someone else. With some effort, she turned her thoughts away from her family and dialed the Grahams' house. This was one family she knew she could call as late as midnight and still find someone up studying or reading.

"Hello, Graham crackers' residence," a boy's voice said. "We're all Grahams here, but not all crackers."

"Hey, Jonah. It's Katelyn. Is Leah there?" Leah's twin brothers may have sounded alike, but their personalities always gave away their identities. Jonah was the joker. Joshua was quieter, rarely answering the phone.

"Hey, Katelyn, I was just thinking about you."

"Of course you were," she said, trying not to smile.

"No seriously. See, I'm working on a project on the Middle East, and Leah said your mom had lived there for a few years. Do you think I could talk to her sometime?"

"So you've been thinking about my mother?" Katelyn asked, teasing.

"Yes. You. Your mom. Whatever. Seriously, though, what do you think? I did my research, but it's missing something. I'm looking for the personal experience to add some depth and put some faces on the statistics."

"Okay, you're doing that thing again. Where you make me feel like I'm talking to my father about his work. Come back down to my level," Katelyn said impatiently. The Graham children were all exceptionally bright, but they had also learned to fit in—which just meant their formidable vocabularies and unique thought processes were usually well-hidden by their social giftedness.

"Will you ask your mom if I can talk to her?" Jonah asked.

"Sure. I know my mom would love to hear about your project and to help in any way she can. But I warn you, once you get her started talking about the Middle East, you'll have trouble shutting her up."

"Great!" Jonah said. "Hang on." He placed his hand over the receiver and yelled, "Leah! Katelyn's on the phone." Then he turned back to Katelyn, saying, "So, while we're waiting for her, what did you do today?"

She smiled. "I went bowling."

"Cool. What was your best score?" he asked. "Oh, never mind. Here's Leah."

"Hey Katelyn," Leah said, her voice warm with affection. "Now scram," she said to Jonah.

"Hi, Leah. How are you?" Remembering how she had felt in the bowling alley that afternoon, Katelyn really wanted to know how her friend was.

"I'm doing okay, I guess. Some days I cry half the morning. Then something good happens or I have a cheerful thought, and I feel grateful to be alive. Noah writes me notes telling me things will get better." Leah sighed.

Katelyn felt relief. "So you regret having the abortion?" The words were out before she thought about them. Why else would Leah be crying?

"No," Leah said, almost immediately. "That's one decision I don't regret."

There was a silence while Katelyn struggled to know what to say next.

"Would it would mean something to you if I was sorry for that?" Leah asked.

"Yes, I guess it would. Why do you cry then?"

Leah laughed. "I ask myself that a lot. Sometimes it's because I feel my life has changed so much. I miss the old days, when I felt safe. Sometimes I'm angry at Carter; other days I feel sorry for him. But enough about me. What's happening with you?"

Katelyn wasn't quite ready to change the subject. "I don't know. This afternoon we all went bowling—Max, Mom, Shawn's family, me and Rachel."

"Sounds like fun."

"Yeah, it was, mostly." Katelyn wanted to tell Leah what had happened at the bowling alley. She wanted to ask Leah whether she got scared and how she faced that fear, to tell her it was an amazing thing that Leah was coping as well as she was instead of locking herself in her room and having a breakdown.

Instead, she asked, "Do you know anything else about when Carter will go to court?"

"Not really. Right now his lawyer has ordered a psychological evaluation. But Elaine says that even though we all have to be ready for the case to go to court, she believes it won't come to that." Elaine was Leah's lawyer.

"What do you mean?"

"She believes Carter's lawyer will try to make a deal. She thinks it will be better for Carter to confess in exchange for a reduced sentence."

"You mean he might be out in a few years?" Katelyn asked, incredulous.

"No, maybe a couple less decades, Katelyn. Elaine says that the charges against him are serious enough that he could end up facing a sentence almost as long as he would live—if he doesn't plea bargain."

Katelyn was quiet so long that Leah finally spoke again, "So is that all you called about?"

"No. No, it isn't. I wondered if you could come over tomorrow afternoon."

"Yeah, sure." Katelyn recognized a smile in her friend's voice.

"Okay, then. See you around one."

"See you," Leah said, then hung up the phone.

Katelyn stood in the dark kitchen for a moment, then turned and went up to her room. She was smiling as she crawled into bed.

CHAPTER 7

A week later as she sat in her Friday afternoon study hall with Shawn, Katelyn was still thinking about that Sunday she had invited Leah over. What had gone wrong? The time had started pleasantly enough with the girls watching a romantic comedy on television. The movie was about a man who was pursuing a woman, and the funny things that happened along the way. Katelyn thought Leah had enjoyed the movie as much as she had. But when it was over, Leah had said something about the story only being funny from the man's point of view. She thought the man's persistence had a dark side and that he should have respected the woman's right to say no to his advances.

"Not everything is about you and Carter," Katelyn had said, too quickly.

Leah had looked shocked, but she held her tongue. Then she shrugged and said, "Let's see what else is on television." For the rest of the afternoon, the girls had watched television, mostly not speaking. They had said an awkward goodbye that day and had not talked since.

Then, this morning at breakfast, Dad had suggested that she and Rachel could invite a girlfriend to spend the night if they wanted.

"Really?" Rachel had squealed. "I'll ask Hillary today at school. Tonight's okay? Right?"

Dad had nodded, pleased his offer had had such a dramatic effect. Katelyn wondered if he knew that when he moved out of the house, the girls had stopped having sleep-overs with their friends. Before then, sleep-overs had occurred at least monthly, mostly between Rachel and Hillary or Katelyn and Leah.

"What about you, Katelyn?" Dad asked, getting up to clear the table.

"No," she had said.

"I bet Leah would love to come," Rachel said. "She hasn't been to Dad's yet."

"You're right," Katelyn said, then turned away from Rachel. "Maybe another time, Dad. I'd rather not invite her right now."

"Why not?" Rachel persisted.

"It's none of your business." Katelyn wasn't going to explain herself to her sister.

"Well, then, I'll have to entertain you myself," Dad said. "Maybe you'd like me to check out slides of invertebrates from the faculty library."

She stared at him in disbelief. Rachel burst out laughing.

"Just kidding, Katelyn. How about a game of Canadian Trivial Pursuit?" Because her dad was Canadian, he liked his daughters to know as much about his country as he could teach them.

"Sounds good. And, Dad?"

"Good one about threatening to check out slides from the faculty library."

He chuckled. "I was beginning to worry you had lost your sense of humor."

But now in study hall, Shawn was talking to her. "Katelyn, you need to get back to work. We've got that government test coming up next week, and you haven't even read half the assignment."

She looked at him, then down at her book. "You could look at it that way. Or you could say, 'Katelyn, good for you. You've read half the assignment already!'"

His expression showed he wasn't buying it. "Yeah, okay. You've read two chapters in three weeks, and you've got two more to read and learn in three days."

"Piece of cake."

"Turn the page."

"I'm not finished reading this page," Katelyn said.

"C'mon. I've been waiting twenty minutes for you to turn the page of that textbook and see what's on the next page."

Curious, Katelyn turned the page and found a folded, single piece of paper. She looked at Shawn, then at the letter addressed to him. The look on his face was proud, happy. It should be good news, she told herself, as the words of "acceptance" and "scholarship" blurred together on the page. She had not missed the most important thing as she scooted her chair back and stood up, bolting toward the restrooms. She had not missed that the letter was from Iowa State University's College of Engineering.

By the time Katelyn had forced herself to stop crying and washed her face, she had rehearsed what she needed to say to Shawn. She braced herself as she pushed open the restroom door. But she wasn't prepared for him to be waiting for her. He put his arms around her, hugging her against him, and the warmth of his welcome started her crying again.

He didn't ask her what was wrong. He just waited, rubbing her arm, standing beside her, letting her curl her face into his shoulder.

Finally, Katelyn could speak. "It's just . . . so far away."

"I know. I know. I know," Shawn said soothingly. "We'll find a way to see each other, Katelyn. We'll find a way to make it work."

"But how can you be sure?" she asked.

"Because I want it to be true. And, we can make it true."

"But you'll get busy and meet other people, and the promises you make now won't mean anything to you when you're gone."

Shawn pulled away from her. "You mean me? Or do you mean Nathan?"

Katelyn didn't know what she meant.

"We—you and me—are going to graduate this year, Katelyn. We are both going to college. This is something we've known since the beginning. And, we've also known it wasn't likely we would go to the same college. But what happens next is up to us. Just make sure of one thing, Katelyn. You owe me this much—never confuse me with Nathan."

Shawn had gone back to their study table and gathered up his books. She had followed him, doing the same. Without another word, he had reached for her hand. Together they had walked to her next class. As she stood watching him walk away to his class, part of her wanted to call after him to come back so she could tell him she was sorry she'd been so selfish, that she was proud of him for getting into Iowa State. But another part of her wanted to scream at him that he wasn't going far enough—that he should go to California, or New Zealand, or China—as far away from her as he could possibly go, because he obviously didn't want to be close to her.

Shawn didn't find Katelyn later in the day, as he often did, which just made her more insecure—and miserable. Her head was throbbing intensely as she drove Rachel and Hillary to Dad's apartment. There the two younger girls began assembling a pizza, while Katelyn turned the lights off in the living room, set the television volume on very low so the voices hummed, and stretched out on the couch, face down. Dad was clearing off the kitchen table so they could eat dinner there.

Katelyn considered taking a shower, but it seemed like too much effort. If she lay very still, she could almost convince herself the pain was gone—at least momentarily. She heard a door creak open, then footsteps as Dad joined her.

"What's the matter, honey?" he asked.

She turned her head toward him. She couldn't exactly see him, just his kneecaps. "I've got a headache," she said.

"Did you take anything for it?"

"Four extra strength pain relievers in two hours."

Dad sniffed, crouching down to her level to look her in the eye. "No more of those until tomorrow, okay?"

"Deal. Any other bright ideas?"

"Do you have your period?"

"No. But it's due . . ." Katelyn stopped and groaned. "In a day or two."

"Those blasted hormones," Dad said, shaking his head. He said that just before her period, the fluctuations of her hormones made Katelyn more susceptible to headaches.

"Anything else?" he asked, starting to rub the knots out of her neck and shoulders.

"Like what?"

"You know. Added stress?"

Katelyn thought for a moment. She opened her mouth, closed it again, pushing down the thoughts and feelings that were bubbling up for relief. Finally, she said, "No, Dad. Nothing out of the ordinary." She turned toward him, awkwardly patting his shoulder. Since he could no longer easily reach her back, he must have thought she was dismissing him and he walked away. Katelyn wanted to call him back, she needed him close. She felt the tears in her eyes, but then he was back.

"Brace yourself, sweetheart," Dad said. "This will be awfully cold." Then he set a flexible ice pack across the back of her neck, adjusting it upward to constrict the blood vessels to her head.

Katelyn gasped at first, feeling her whole body tense from the shock. Then she felt the warmth of her father's hands on her back, coaxing her reluctant muscles to relax. She took a deep breath and let it out, realizing the icy cold on her neck was completely blocking the pain. Gratitude filled her. She was glad for the relief from pain and for her father's presence.

In the morning, Katelyn woke early. Her headache was gone, as was her insecurity about her and Shawn. She felt a sense of optimism about their future. She even felt like calling Leah.

As she showered, Katelyn sang softly. She dressed quickly, pulling on her jeans and sweatshirt. She found her father in the kitchen, reading the paper. He set it down when she came in and slipped his arm around her waist, squeezing her quickly, then letting her go.

"How's the headache this morning?" Dad asked.

"Gone." Katelyn grinned at him.

He smiled and pushed a chair out for her to sit next to him. "That is good news. And, I can see the mood is also good. We're in for a good day, all around, then, I take it?"

"I hope so."

"What are your plans for the day?"

"I need to go see Shawn and Leah."

Dad raised an eyebrow. "Need to?"

Katelyn helped herself to his coffee cup, took a sip, and said, "Yeah, that's right."

"So there is more going on in that head of yours than just hormonal fluctuations."

She laughed. "So it seems."

"There's more coffee, by the way. In case you want your own."

"What you're saying is you'd like yours back."

Dad nodded. "Exactly."

Katelyn got up and poured herself a half cup of

coffee, then filled the rest of the cup with milk. When she sat back down, she was surprised to see Dad hadn't gone back to reading the paper. He was waiting for her.

She cleared her throat. "Dad?"

He met her eyes.

"What do you do when people make decisions you think are wrong?"

"Happens all the time," he said. "People vote for the wrong politicians, who give environmental concessions to big business, and . . ."

Katelyn stopped him. "I was thinking more about people you know well—your friends, for example."

He considered for a moment. "Do you mean 'wrong' or do you mean decisions I just don't like?"

"Let's start with wrong."

"Wrong meaning that someone gets hurt?"

She nodded.

"I could tell them why I think they're making a bad decision."

"And, if that doesn't work?"

"I try not to judge them."

"Aren't some things always wrong?"

"You know, I used to think so. Take divorce. How can divorce always be wrong when the reasons people get married in the first place are so screwed up?

Some people get married for love, don't get me wrong. But some people just want to leave home or have sex or have children. Or they believe this may be their only chance at happiness. Or they want financial security. Does God really want to bless all marriages?"

Katelyn was listening so hard, she almost couldn't respond. She was trying to substitute other words for divorce. Like abortion. Would her father say that abortion couldn't always be wrong either because the reasons people had sex in the first place were also screwed up?

"What about sex?" she asked. She couldn't ask about abortion. That was too close to revealing Leah's secret.

"What about it?" he asked.

"Is sex outside of marriage always wrong?"

Dad was quiet for a long moment. "If I have to answer honestly, Katelyn, I don't believe sex outside of marriage is always wrong."

"But . . ."

"No, let me explain. I believe that sex outside of a loving relationship is wrong. It can create all kinds of problems—unwanted pregnancies and sexually transmitted diseases, to name two. These are problems that are difficult to face alone, but if the relationship isn't solid, one person may be left very alone to face these problems."

Katelyn nodded. Carter and Leah's relationship had appeared to be loving, at least for a time. If they had gotten married though, would that have changed the nature of the relationship? Would Carter have been able to help Leah face the pregnancy, or would he merely have used the child to hold on more tightly to Leah?

"Okay, so here's the other side of this. When I say that sex needs to happen in the context of a loving relationship, I'm also applying that standard to marriage."

She frowned. "So, you're saying that marriage . . ."

"Isn't permission to have sex. Exactly. Unless the marriage is also experienced as a loving relationship by both partners, the sex act is diminished."

"The sex act, Dad?"

He blushed. "Well, I am a scientist, first and foremost."

"But even so, saying it's diminished is not the same thing as saying it's wrong, once and for all."

"Okay. You're right. I believe it's wrong for two people who are married to have sex if they do not love each other. Clear enough?"

Katelyn was silent for a moment, absorbing the information.

"You're not thinking of having sex, are you?" Dad asked then, almost shyly. He ran his finger back and forth across the edge of the folded newspaper in front of him.

Still preoccupied, she shook her head no.

He let out a big sigh. "Good! Because you know, since you're my daughter, it's always wrong for you to have sex. At least until I give you my permission."

Katelyn grinned. "Yeah, I'm sure I'll be calling you up late on my wedding night asking for your blessing."

"Well, if I let you get married, then you don't have to ask."

The two smiled at each other. Then Katelyn grew serious again. "But Dad, what you believe isn't exactly what I thought you would say—as a Mennonite, I mean."

He nodded. "I stand with Mennonites on many issues, Katelyn. But as I've gotten older, I've realized that personal relationships, marriage, and sexuality are much more complex issues than my parents taught me. I'm still trying to figure out my beliefs, sorting through what I was taught and who I am. You'll find this too, as you get older, that understanding oneself takes on new dimensions and raises questions you can't anticipate."

Katelyn thought she must already be getting older. She got up from the table. "Well, all this talking has made me hungry. Whose job is it to make breakfast around here anyway?"

"Whoever asks the question, probably," he said, opening the fridge door. "Seriously, though, I've got bacon, eggs, toast . . ." he said, handing her each item as he named it.

"Your fridge makes toast?"

"Bread."

"Your fridge makes bread? That's incredible."

"I can tell I'll never recover from this. Anyway, there are all kinds of great breakfast foods, including fruit. I bought everything I could think of."

Katelyn peeked into the fridge and laughed. "You'd think we're going to have breakfast three times today."

"We just might. But right now, it's just us two. Our two best buds aren't likely to be up before ten, so I'm not cooking for them yet."

The telephone rang then, startling Katelyn. "What time is it anyway?"

"Eight exactly," Dad said, handing her the telephone.

"Hello," Katelyn said automatically into the receiver, while rolling her eyes at her dad.

"Hey, Katelyn, it's me, Shawn. I was hoping you'd be up."

"We get up early around here," she said. "Shawn, I am so sorry about yesterday. I am really proud of you for being accepted at Iowa. I don't want to be selfish about you." She pulled the telephone cord as tight as it would go, to allow her to get around the corner of the kitchen doorway. It was an illusion of privacy, but her father was whistling loudly over the sound of bacon beginning to fry.

"Thanks, Katelyn. It's okay. I could have broken the news to you more gently. I just wasn't thinking it would seem that far away to you."

"And, I shouldn't have been thinking so much about myself, Shawn. It's your choice, your future."

He was quiet for a moment. "You're my choice, too, Katelyn. I want to talk about what we're going to do this fall when we're apart to help us stay close. But first, to show you how important this is to me, I want you to visit the campus with me this summer."

"Really? You'd do that for me?" She was grinning from ear to ear.

He chuckled. "Not for you. With you. Oh, and probably my parents—one or both of them."

"Yes, I'd love that. I mean, if it's okay with my parents."

"Great. It's a plan."

"Shawn?"

"Yes?"

"Do you want to do something this evening?"

"Sure, what did you have in mind?"

"First I have to finish studying for that test . . ."

"Yeah, I was going to remind you."

"But then maybe we could do something with Rachel and Jason."

"Like what?" Shawn asked.

"I don't know. Something different. Maybe make dinner together or go to a park?"

"We could do both. Make sandwiches and have a picnic at a park. I could bring a Frisbee. How about we meet you at your mom's house around five?"

"Yeah, that'll work. You could bring your dog Sophie too," Katelyn suggested.

Shawn laughed. "If I do that, we'll spend most of our time running after her, you realize?"

"I can live with that," Katelyn said. "See you then." She hung up the phone, smiling. Now she just had to call Leah.

"Bacon, eggs, toast are all ready," Dad said, handing her a plate. "Want to play Trivial Pursuit while we eat, since we didn't get to last night?"

"Sure!" Katelyn raced out of the kitchen to get the game.

By the time Rachel and Hillary woke up, it was almost noon. Katelyn and Dad had long finished their game. Katelyn had caught up on the reading for her government test, and Dad had graded most of his students' papers. After lunch, Katelyn and Rachel dropped Hillary off at her house and headed home.

"I talked to Shawn this morning before you got up. He and Jason are coming over tonight, unless you've got other plans," Katelyn said.

Rachel smiled. "No other plans. That will be great to see them."

When they got home, Rachel went grocery shopping with Mom. Katelyn called Leah's house. Her mom answered.

"Hi Ginger. It's Katelyn. Is Leah there?"

"Um. She's a bit busy right now. I've got her making spaghetti sauce in the kitchen. Can she call you back in a bit?"

"Sure." Katelyn felt a little doubtful, but shrugged it off.

The afternoon passed quickly as Katelyn finished her homework and cleaned her room. Shawn and

Jason arrived promptly at five. Rachel let them in, as Katelyn sprinted down the stairs from her room.

"Did you bring Sophie?" she asked, breathless.

Shawn laughed. "Yeah, she's in the car going crazy. We went ahead and packed a cooler since she can't be alone in the car very long by herself. You two ready to go?"

The telephone rang just as Katelyn said, "Yes." The girls looked at each other. "I'll get it," Rachel said, slipping into her shoes before turning toward the kitchen.

Katelyn grabbed their jackets from the closet.

"Katelyn!" Rachel called. "It's for you."

She gave Rachel her jacket and took the telephone.

"Hello?"

"Katelyn. It's me, Noah."

Not now, Katelyn thought, glancing at Shawn, who was waiting. Jason and Rachel were on their way out to the car.

"I want to know what's going on between you and Leah," Noah said, getting straight to the point.

"What do you mean?" Katelyn said, turning to walk back to the kitchen and leaving Shawn without any explanation. This phone call didn't have to take long, she thought. "I called her today."

"Why aren't you camped out in her room, helping her get through this? Remember when Bradshaw died? She couldn't stand it. That dog had adored her all his life. She couldn't bear to walk around the house. Everywhere she saw him, found a memory of them being together. You stayed with her, sleeping in her room for three days, shadowing her like he did, letting her talk your ear off about what a great dog he'd been, writing down everything she said about him so she'd never forget him. I couldn't believe how patient you were with her."

Katelyn bit her lip.

"Remember?" Noah demanded.

"Yes." Her face burned, and she felt shame. Why wasn't this situation the same as that? Hadn't Leah lost more than a dog?

"How old were you then?"

"Thirteen."

"God, Katelyn . . ." he choked. "I would have given my right arm for a friend like you. You amazed me."

"Really?" She was surprised.

But Noah wasn't finished. He continued, angry now, "Where is that friend now, when Leah needs you so much more?"

Katelyn was silent, brooding. She didn't know

how to answer him. She didn't like the feeling that she owed him an explanation.

"You still love her, don't you, Katelyn?" he asked. His voice was pleading. She felt herself softening.

"Of course."

"Then you have to get over being mad at her for . . . the abortion. You just have to."

"But I . . ." she began.

"No. No 'but's." Again his tone was decisive, bossy. She felt her temper rising, but when he spoke again, his voice was soft and she could hear his tears. "You're breaking her heart, Katelyn. Please don't do that to her, not now."

Then he hung up the phone.

CHAPTER 8

In the week after Noah's call, Katelyn thought a lot about what he had said. But she didn't try to call Leah. She had left the message with Ginger for Leah to call her when she was finished making spaghetti sauce. Katelyn figured the next move was Leah's. For all she knew, Leah was still in the kitchen, trapped by mountainous quarts of the sauce.

On the Thursday afternoon before Easter, Katelyn returned home from school to find a message on the answering machine from Jonah.

"Hey, Katelyn. It's me, Jonah Graham. Have you

had a chance to ask your mom if I could talk to her about the Middle East? I haven't been working on my paper for a while, but I want to finish it up next week. Call me back."

Katelyn shook her head. She had completely forgotten. She dialed her mom's number at work to ask her, then called Jonah to apologize.

"Sorry, Jonah," she said right away when he answered the phone. "I forgot to give my mom the message."

"It's okay. Happens around here all the time," he said cheerfully.

"I messed up."

He laughed. "Really, it's no big deal. If I'd needed it, I would have called before now and asked again."

"Well, she said her schedule's pretty open this weekend. She suggested Saturday since tomorrow's Good Friday."

"How about Saturday after lunch?" he asked. "Do you want me to come over?"

"No. I'll bring her to your house," Katelyn said, feeling it was the least she could do.

"Okay, great. See you around two, if that works for you."

"Sure." As Katelyn hung up, Rachel burst in the door.

"Hey," she called out happily.

"Hey back," Katelyn said. "Are you packed?"

"Not yet. When's Dad coming again?"

Katelyn looked at her watch. "He said he'd be here by five. So you have a half hour."

"I wish he'd wait until Mom got home. I don't like not seeing her before we go. What if something happened to her while we were with Dad?"

"Something like?"

"I don't know. An accident or something. Never mind. I've got to pack." Rachel turned and ran upstairs to her room.

Katelyn was surprised. She hadn't realized her sister worried about Mom.

When they got to Dad's apartment, he insisted the girls be in bed by ten. He had plans for them for Good Friday and said they'd have to be up by seven.

"Are we going fishing?" Katelyn had asked.

He laughed. "No, then you'd have to be up by four."

"Golfing then?" Rachel asked.

"Not this time," he said. "But I'll keep that in mind for another time."

"As a punishment," Rachel muttered under her breath.

Katelyn couldn't sleep. She listened to Rachel's

rhythmic breathing in the bed across the room. She liked this, she realized. At her father's apartment, the girls shared a bedroom, for the first time in their lives. Rachel often talked to Katelyn long after they were in bed. But not tonight. Dad had asked them to try to sleep. Katelyn had wanted to talk. She wanted to ask Rachel what else she worried about besides Mom. But Rachel was happy, excited about the surprise their father had planned. And she must have been tired because she fell asleep within minutes.

Katelyn couldn't get to sleep until well after midnight. She couldn't relax. She had too many pictures in her mind. She found herself one minute imagining Carter in jail, and the next seeing Leah fully pregnant—but with no baby inside—standing before a judge. Then an image of Noah popped into her mind, tragically having chosen to live the rest of his life alone, since he couldn't be with Jenna, his one true love. She saw Nathan, frowning as he pored over books in a college library, and wondered if she would feel the same way in the fall. She tried to imagine Shawn in counseling—the two of him, Shawn now and the younger Shawn who had witnessed his real father hurting his mother. She saw Kiana grinning as she rode Trim Jim, galloping through a field, not needing someone to spot her, free somehow to become one with her horse, and Katelyn wondered if this was one of Kiana's dreams. All these images and more danced through Katelyn's mind, first as she lay awake, then gradually, they infiltrated her sleep.

Friday morning came too early for Katelyn. Rachel woke her at seven. She was already dressed and ready to go. Katelyn tried to move quickly, but was still half asleep. When she got to the kitchen, Dad handed her a cup of coffee.

"Ready?" he asked.

She shook her head no.

"Well, let's go," Rachel said. "You can sleep in the car."

"Do you know where we're going?" Katelyn whispered to her sister, as she followed her out to the car.

"Not yet," Rachel said. "Just that we'll be in the car a bit."

Katelyn climbed into the back seat, tucked her coffee into the cup holder, and lay down across the seat. She dozed off and woke up just as her dad slowed the car, turning into the drive of the South Bend Regional Transportation Center.

"We're flying somewhere?" Rachel asked.

"No. Not today. We're taking the train to Chicago for the day. There's a new exhibit on DNA at the Museum of Science and Industry I want to see."

"DNA!" Rachel laughed. "Why didn't you tell me, Dad? I could have invited all my friends at school. Man, they are going to be so jealous when I tell them what I got to do on my long weekend!"

"But I thought. . . ." Dad parked the car, then looked at Rachel's face. "Oh, I get it, you're teasing."

Rachel glanced back at Katelyn and grinned. Dad's enthusiasm for science was contagious. Over the years, he had taken them to the museum in Chicago many times, and the girls had always enjoyed themselves.

"Good choice, Dad," Katelyn said, approving.

"Thanks." Dad got out of the car and went to get something from the trunk. The girls got out more slowly.

"What do you have there?" Rachel asked, pointing to the backpack Dad was holding.

"Snacks and drinks, mostly. I thought about bringing something for each of us to read, but I ran out of time."

"We don't need reading material, Dad," Rachel said, taking his arm. "Not when we have you."

"Yeah, we'll need that intro lecture on genetics this morning so we can understand what we're seeing," Katelyn chimed in, taking the backpack from him as she took his other arm.

"Anything for my two young budding scientists," Dad said, grinning from ear to ear.

The day in Chicago was a great success. The two-hour train ride passed quickly, with the girls ravenously devouring the snacks in the first hour. The trio spent the full day at the museum, stopping only to eat lunch. At the end of the day, they each picked out a souvenir in the gift shop, before heading back to the train station for the ride home. Katelyn chose a bracelet with pretty white stones, while Rachel wanted one just like it only with blue stones. Dad picked out a book on the DNA exhibit, then found a book for Rachel on the physiology of dance and one for Katelyn on the healing effect of animals.

She looked at him quizzically when he handed her the book.

"There's a chapter on horses," he explained. "I thought it would interest you because of your work at Redbud with the children."

Katelyn was touched. "Yes," she said. "Natalie, the director at Redbud, has been encouraging me to consider studying physical therapy."

"Really?" he asked. "That's a great idea. Or you could study medicine and do research."

"Or you could be president of the United States," Rachel chimed in.

"I was saving that for you, dear," Dad said, laughing. "You could make quite a name for yourself as the first ballerina to go into politics!"

They walked back to the train station, buying sandwiches at a deli to eat on the train. They talked the whole way home, interrupting each other excitedly as if, Katelyn thought, they wanted to make the experience last as long as possible. When Dad came into their room to say goodnight, Katelyn had wrapped her arms around his neck, kissed his cheek, and said, "Dad, this is the most fun we've had since you moved out."

He looked at her. "Yes," he said. "I suppose it is. We'll have to do it again soon."

"And, maybe we could bring Jason and Shawn next time?" Rachel asked.

"Sure," he said. "Do they like science?"

"Well, we don't always have to go to the science museum," Katelyn said. "There are lots of amazing places to go in Chicago."

"You're right," Dad said, moving toward Rachel, but still looking at Katelyn. "If you ever graduate from high school, that might be one way to celebrate—by taking the four of you kids to Chicago."

"Make that 'when,'" she said. "And, you may want to start saving for it now."

Saturday morning, Katelyn heard her dad get up around four-thirty and met him in the kitchen. The two sat at the table reading and drinking coffee. When the newspaper was delivered at five, Katelyn took the sections she wanted to read first and handed the rest to her father.

It wasn't until two o'clock, when Katelyn and her mother stood in front of Leah's house, Katelyn realized how tired she was.

Jonah opened the door and held out his hand to Mom. "Mrs. Neufeld, thanks so much for coming. Hi Katelyn."

"Hi Jonah. You can call me Liz," Mom said, taking his hand graciously. "I brought some photos in case you're interested."

He beamed. "Great. We'll work at the dining room table." He led the way for her to follow. Katelyn, at a loss for what to do, also followed them to the table. Jonah had a pad of paper with questions written on it and a tape recorder.

"Mom, Mrs. Neufeld is here. I think we're ready," Jonah called.

"Be right there," she called back.

He turned back to them. "Mom wants to evaluate how I interview you so she's going to listen."

"What a great idea!" Mom said.

Jonah turned to Katelyn. "Leah's up in her room. She said you're welcome to hang out with her."

"Thanks," Katelyn said, slipping off her coat and turning to go. Her mom also slipped off her jacket, which Katelyn was about to take, when Jonah snatched them out of their hands.

"Sorry," he said. "I was so excited about you're being here, I forgot my manners." He went to the closet to hang them up while Katelyn slowly climbed the stairs to Leah's room.

The door was open, but Katelyn hesitated, noticing the many piles of books, posters, and clothes. A few boxes were strewn about, but it was impossible to tell whether they were being unpacked or packed.

"Leah?" she said uncertainly.

"Katelyn, come on in."

As she turned to the sound of the voice, Katelyn realized that Leah was sitting on the floor behind the bed, almost hidden from view. She picked her way across the room and plopped down on the bed, which was the only clear surface.

"Hey, Leah. How are you?" Katelyn asked, taking in her friend, who was still wearing her pajamas and had her arms wrapped around a large stuffed grey hippo, a favorite gift from Noah on her eleventh birthday.

Leah looked at her and tried to smile. "I . . . ," she said, then stopped.

Katelyn knew immediately why her friend couldn't finish the sentence. She either didn't know how she was or she didn't want to lie. Katelyn slipped off the bed and into a place on the floor next to Leah. "What are you doing?" she asked, putting her arm around Leah.

Immediately, Leah moved closer, laying her head on Katelyn's shoulder. "I'm sorting my things. I've outgrown a bunch of them. I was packing them up for Daddy to give away. But then Mom said we should just put them in the attic for now. She's afraid I'll change my mind."

"Umm," Katelyn said, settling more into her place beside Leah.

A quiet settled over the room between the two girls. Katelyn could hear the hum of voices below them. She closed her eyes and listened, taking in the sounds of squirrels scolding, birds calling, cars driving by. After a while, she began to want to get up, but she waited because Leah was still quiet and relaxed.

"Mom told me today you called a couple of weeks

ago when I was making spaghetti sauce," Leah said finally.

"Sorry?" Katelyn was confused.

"Today, when Jonah was making cookies for your mom, all of the sudden Mom remembered you had called me a few weeks ago. So I got your message today."

Katelyn didn't say anything. She felt badly that she had been telling herself it was Leah's turn to call her, since she had made the first move.

"It made me feel better," Leah said.

"I'm glad."

"But it would have made me feel even better if you'd tried to call me again."

"You could have called me," Katelyn said.

"Lately, it's been hard to know if you wanted to see me."

Katelyn wasn't sure either, but she didn't want to dwell on that right now. "I'm here now."

Leah pulled away and grinned at her. "Just in time to help me finish cleaning up this mess."

"I'd be happy to—after you have a shower and get dressed."

"Next thing you know, you'll be telling me I have to brush my teeth," Leah said, standing up and swatting at Katelyn.

"What a great idea!" Katelyn exclaimed. "Did you think of that all by yourself?"

Leah set her hippo gently on her bed and took some clothes off one of the piles. "While I'm gone, you can put these things back in the dresser. Everything else goes in the boxes." She pointed out the piles to keep, which were all against the walls of the room.

"So you don't care where I put things in the dresser as long as I keep the piles together?" Katelyn asked, realizing that Leah's chaotic room was actually highly organized.

"Right." Leah nodded and swept out of the room.

When Leah returned less than ten minutes later, Katelyn had finished with the dresser and was beginning to fill the boxes. Leah looked cheerful in a bright turquoise t-shirt and blue jeans, as if she could face the day, and any number of days that lay ahead. Her dark brown curls were still streaked with maroon, pulled back in a ponytail.

"You look so . . ."

"Clean?" Leah finished.

"Energetic."

Leah nodded. "I have my moments. Unfortunately, most of the time, I sit around and 'do nothing.'" She made quotation marks in the air with her fingers. "Mom thinks I'm depressed. And," she shrugged, "maybe I am. But I don't see it that way. I'm sorting things out in here," she tapped her head.

After the girls had put everything in its place, they went downstairs to check on the interview. The mothers were sitting and talking at the table with the twins. The interview appeared to be over.

"How did he do?" Leah asked Katelyn's mom, reaching for the plate of cookies sitting between her and Jonah and holding it out for Katelyn.

"He was fantastic," Mom said, smiling.

"Yes, he was," Ginger agreed.

Katelyn noticed Jonah's blush.

"He practices all the time," Joshua said. "He asks us questions, then asks us if they're good questions."

"Following in Noah's footsteps," Leah said.

"Unfortunately, he doesn't get to practice much with people outside the family, although he has interviewed a few people at church and written articles for the church newsletter," Ginger said.

"Well, it was fun," Mom said, standing up. "Thanks, Jonah, for asking me."

"When I've got the story written, will you read it and make sure it's accurate?" he asked.

"Sure. You can e-mail it to me." She scribbled her address down for him at the top of his pad of paper.

"Good cookies," Katelyn said to Jonah. "Leah said you made them."

"I put some in a bag for you to take home," he said. "Just in case you didn't get down here in time to have some."

"Aww," Katelyn said, squeezing his shoulder.

Later that evening, Katelyn sat on the couch with Shawn trying to read the subtitles of a foreign movie he had brought over for them to watch together. She was having trouble following the story line, and her mind kept wandering back to her time with Leah. They had gotten along so well, but she wondered how Leah was really doing.

When the movie ended, Shawn turned off the television and pulled Katelyn closer to him.

"I had an appointment with my counselor Jeff this week," he said.

"Oh. How did that go?" she asked.

"My mom went with me. She talked about how life was with my real father." He shook his head. "He was pretty messed up."

Katelyn squeezed his hand, hoping he would continue.

"I think that's why my older brother Thomas has it harder than me. He just remembers more fights. So he drinks. Generally, I've got less to forget. And, life with my stepdad has been good." Shawn shook his head again and sniffed. "Jeff wants me to understand I have choices about what kind of person I'll be."

"But you're nothing like your real dad. I mean . . ."

"Actually. In some ways, I am like him. I wish I wasn't. But I am. I'm realizing that it's okay to be like him, as long as I don't act like him."

"I don't get it."

"It's okay for me to get mad, like when Carter was threatening you and Leah. But instead of hauling off and using my fists, Jeff wants me to think of other ways of handling situations that are more respectful of the other person—even if the person doesn't appear to be worthy of respect."

"Is Jeff Mennonite?" Katelyn asked.

Shawn smiled. "I thought the same thing myself. No, but he said he goes to one of the other peace churches—Church of the Brethren, I think."

"Is he trying to convert you?"

"No, that's not the feeling I get. He wants me to understand and accept myself."

"And choose."

"Right. Decide who I want to be . . . sort of like, when I grow up."

"I think you're growing up just fine," Katelyn said, leaning in to kiss him.

He allowed one long kiss, then stood up. "Glad you think so, Katelyn. But I think I'd better get going. You're going to the sunrise service tomorrow, last I knew. And it's getting late."

"Yes, I am. It's my favorite." Katelyn stood up, too.

"Better than Christmas?" He kissed her gently on her forehead.

"Oh yeah. For me, anyway. Just when you thought there was no hope, it's given back to you—bigger than you'd dared to believe."

"Are you talking about Pandora's box? Or the resurrection?" Shawn asked, laughing.

Katelyn laughed, too. "I guess it could have been either."

"You and Rachel are still coming over tomorrow afternoon?"

"If you and Jason will have us."

"Well, I can't speak for him, but I'll keep up my end of the bargain," Shawn said, looking into her eyes. Then he leaned over to kiss her again.

The next morning, after the sunrise service, Katelyn was washing dishes in the church's kitchen after the breakfast when she sensed someone standing next to her.

"Hey, Katelyn," Nathan said quietly, setting a stack of plates on the counter.

"Hi, Nathan." She turned to look at him, but he had already taken a few steps away from her. The pastor, Russell, was clasping him on the arm and talking to him so Katelyn went back to washing dishes. She felt uneasy, as if there were something she wanted to tell him, but she couldn't remember.

Instead, she put her energy into scrubbing first the plates and silverware, then the pots and pans. By the time she was done, only a handful of people were left, picking up stray bulletins, stacking the last chairs, and finishing up their conversations. Katelyn assumed Nathan had gone home.

"We'll meet you in the car," Rachel called to Katelyn in the kitchen.

Katelyn nodded. "I just have to get my purse." But she couldn't find her purse in the sanctuary. She started down the hall to check the bathroom when she heard Nathan's voice, coming soft and low from behind the pastor's closed office door.

"She wanted sex from me, that was all, Russell," Nathan said. He sounded agonized.

She was shocked. That wasn't true. Then Katelyn realized he wasn't talking about her. She knew she shouldn't listen, but she couldn't help it. There was so much about Nathan she didn't understand.

"I mean, she did everything possible to get my attention when school started. And I got completely caught up in it. She seemed so sweet—and serious about her faith. Everyone liked her. I was infatuated with her, I just forgot about everything. Then she invited me home for Thanksgiving. I thought she must really like me because she wanted me to meet her parents. But when we got there, her parents weren't home. And, she came on to me. . . . At first, she was playful and affectionate, but then I realized we were going farther than I wanted to and tried to get her to stop. But she wouldn't. Instead, she just tried harder, and she taunted me. It was awful. She was so intense, I felt intimidated. I didn't know how to get out of it. I . . . I gave in."

Katelyn bit her lip so hard she tasted blood. He gave in? He gave in. The words echoed in her head. Then it dawned on her: Nathan was talking about the beginning of this school year. This girl was the reason he'd never written or called Katelyn as he had promised last summer.

Russell cleared his throat. "What happened next, son?"

"I felt awful. I hated her, hated myself. I lay

awake all night. In the morning, I left. Took a cab from her house to the bus station. Caught the bus back to Kansas."

Katelyn heard Nathan sniff a couple of times and knew he was fighting for control. She wondered if he was hurt or angry.

"Back at school, when I was around her, it was confusing. She seemed sweet and good, but it was nothing personal. She wasn't interested in me anymore. Don't get me wrong. I was relieved about that. I just wanted to get home, back to Katelyn."

Katelyn was startled, then her anger flared up. Nathan had sex with another girl, then had come home and wanted Katelyn to marry him! She put her hand on the doorknob, but Russell's voice stopped her.

"You wanted to be with Katelyn because things didn't work out with the other girl?" Russell asked. Katelyn knew he was baiting Nathan, forcing him to explain that things were not as ridiculous as they appeared.

"No. I wanted to be with Katelyn because I trust her, and I hadn't understood how valuable that was before. But I messed up . . ."

Out of the corner of her eye, Katelyn saw movement. She turned to see Rachel through the glass door at the end of the hallway motioning her to come. In one hand, Rachel was holding up the purse. Quietly, Katelyn turned and crept down the hall, pushed open the door, and walked with her sister to the car.

"What on earth were you doing outside Pastor Russell's door?" Rachel asked.

"Eavesdropping."

"On who?"

"It doesn't matter," Katelyn said. "I can't talk about it."

Another secret to keep, she thought. If only she could tell Leah. Somehow this would all make sense to her. Then Leah could explain it to Katelyn. She rubbed her forehead. She didn't want to tell Leah anything, she realized. If they hadn't been such good friends in the first place, Katelyn would not have been the one to drive Leah to the abortion clinic. Katelyn could have stayed blissfully ignorant, as in the dark as Leah had left her parents. She rubbed her head again. She hated secrets.

CHAPTER 9

On the afternoon of Easter Sunday, Katelyn and Rachel stood on the doorstep of the Roberts' house. Rachel rang the doorbell. Sophie started barking excitedly. Katelyn heard Shawn calling the dog and a scramble of footsteps.

"We need a dog," Rachel said, grinning.

"Yeah, let's add that to the list of things to ask Mom for."

The door was yanked open and there was Jason, a mischievous grin on his face. "Come in. Come in."

Katelyn glanced curiously at Rachel, but her

sister was already inside. Jason held out his hands to take their jackets.

"Hello, girls!" Mrs. Roberts called out from the living room. "I'll be in shortly. Shawn's getting Sophie settled in the basement."

Rachel started toward the living room, but Jason pulled her back. "Wait."

Mrs. Roberts came around the corner, eyes bright. "Good afternoon, girls. Happy Easter." She kissed each of them on the cheek. Katelyn was touched. Her mother would never kiss one of her friends, not Shawn, nor Leah. It just wasn't her style.

"Sorry to keep you standing here. But you see, you can't come in yet," she said. "We've got to wait for Shawn. This was all his idea." She was wringing her hands quickly back and forth as if she could hardly wait herself.

Katelyn looked at Rachel, who shrugged, then at Jason, grinning ear to ear. Then Katelyn heard Shawn's footsteps running up from the basement, the door creaking shut. Sophie whimpered softly as Shawn crossed the kitchen floor and into the hall. Then he stood in front of them.

"Happy Easter, Katelyn. Rachel." He was grinning, too. "Jason and I have been working on a little treat for you. Mom helped."

His mother chuckled.

"We can tell you're all about to burst," Katelyn said. "So tell us."

"We've put together an Easter egg hunt," Shawn said.

Katelyn laughed. She saw Rachel reach for Jason's hand and give it a squeeze.

"But it's not your usual egg hunt," Shawn said. "The eggs are still white, and we'll color them together after you find them."

"That was my idea," Jason said. "I thought that would be more fun."

"I like it," Rachel said.

"And, there's more. You'll find eggs and chocolates and things that you can easily identify as Easter-related. But Jason and I also hid one special gift for each of you that is relevant to you. If you find your sister's, you have to leave it there for her to find. These gifts are not hidden, but they will look out of place in their surroundings. That will be your clue. Any questions?"

"What does the winner get?" Rachel asked impishly, glancing at Katelyn.

"Good question," Shawn said. "All of the goodies will be divided up equally between you two, but Jason and I are hoping some of the chocolate will be shared with us. The winner will get to be in charge of this sharing."

Katelyn and Rachel giggled.

"Well, kids, have fun. Jim and I will be in the basement if you need us," Mrs. Roberts said, starting toward the kitchen.

"What? You're banished?" Rachel asked.

"Oh, no. I've got my sewing machine down there, and we'll be watching television. Jim's got his newspaper. We're well situated."

"See you later, Mom," Jason said. "You two need to close your eyes."

Both girls immediately closed their eyes, eager to start. Katelyn felt Shawn slip his arm around her waist as he led her into the living room.

"Keep your eyes closed for a moment more," he said, then left her side. When he returned, he placed something in her hand, which she figured out was the handle of a wicker basket.

"Okay, open your eyes," Jason said.

Katelyn opened her eyes. She was facing the fireplace mantel and instantly noticed the slightest hint of white sticking out from behind a family photo. As she started toward it, Rachel was racing toward something she spotted in the dining room.

The girls continued to search. Shawn and Jason

had used the whole main floor of the house as the hiding places for their treats. Some things were easy to find, an egg tucked behind a white curtain. Others were harder, a boxed chocolate bunny turned sideways in the crammed bookshelf. Rachel was the first to find Jason's gift for her—a deck of cards with Captain Kirk on the back and a cribbage board modeled after the Starship Enterprise. She squealed with delight and ran to Jason. "Thanks so much. This is just too cool," she said.

"Where was it?" Katelyn asked, curious. As far as she knew, she had not even gotten close to finding Shawn's gift for her.

"In the bathroom."

Katelyn laughed. "So if the theme hadn't given it away, the location would have."

Jason nodded proudly. "Well, of course. No one plays crib in the bathroom."

"No, just solitaire," Shawn joked. "What do you think, Jason, have they found all the eggs and candy?"

Jason nodded. "I think so. Katelyn, you need to spend some time in the kitchen."

Katelyn put down her loaded basket and went to the kitchen. The other three joined her.

"Cold," Shawn said as she nosed around the

refrigerator. She started across the room to the stove, and Jason said, "Warm, ah, cold."

She backed up until Rachel offered, "Warm." Katelyn looked around. In front of her on the counter was a cookbook open on a bookstand. There were top cupboards and lower cupboards, which all got a "cold" pronouncement. She looked again at the cookbook.

"Hot," Shawn said, grinning.

Katelyn pulled it toward her and realized as she did so that there were two books on the stand. The slender cookbook concealed a second book. She pulled it out and saw the lined pages were blank. She closed the book. The cover picture was a beautiful drawing of a black stallion galloping through a field of blue flowers.

"It's a journal," Shawn explained. Jason motioned to Rachel, and she followed him out of the kitchen.

Katelyn said, "But I don't keep a journal."

"Not yet," he said. "But you might like to someday. My counselor has me writing in one. It helps me sort things out."

She traced her finger over the outline of the horse. "It's a great gift, Shawn," she said, wondering what he wrote in his journal.

He pulled her close. "You know, I'm hoping

someday I'll be the place you come to sort out your thoughts. Sometimes you feel very far away."

She hadn't realized it showed. "Thanks, Shawn."

"We better get in there before Jason and Rachel eat all the best goodies," Shawn said.

"I think I've already got the best, right here," Katelyn murmured, kissing him on the mouth.

That night, when Rachel and Katelyn returned home, Mom and Max were sitting on the couch talking. The girls set down their Easter baskets by the door. Rachel plopped down on the armchair facing them.

"Hey Max, so when are you going to invite us to your place to go horseback riding?" Rachel asked.

Katelyn hung up her coat, scooped the journal out of her basket, and moved closer to listen. She stood behind Rachel, partly in the circle and partly on the outside.

"Have a seat, honey," Mom said, waving at the second armchair across the room.

She shook her head no. "I'm not staying long. I have some things I want to do before I go to bed."

"You didn't answer my question," Rachel prompted Max.

He laughed. "I was waiting for a break in the conversation. I'd be happy for you to come. How about next Saturday?" He glanced at Mom, his eyebrows up, waiting as much for her approval as for Rachel's, Katelyn thought.

"Next Saturday . . ." Rachel's eyes gleamed happily as she pretended to consider it. "I believe I can work that into my schedule. How about you, Katelyn?"

"No. I'll be at Redbud that day," she said, then turned to Max. "But thank you. It's nice of you to invite us."

Rachel looked disappointed. "But you're only there in the morning. You could come. We could go in the afternoon, so you could come along with us."

"One set of stables a day is more than enough for me, thanks." Katelyn did not want to go.

"Awww, c'mon," Rachel pleaded.

"It's okay, Rachel," Mom said. "We'll get Katelyn to come out another time."

Katelyn shot her mother an angry glare. Mom said nothing, but tilted her chin in the air.

"Rachel," Max said. "Why don't you bring one of your friends?"

Rachel nodded. "Really? Could I?"

"Sure."

"That could be even more fun than if Katelyn came along," Rachel said pointedly.

"Fine," Katelyn said, tugging lightly on her sister's hair and leaving.

Up in her bedroom, Katelyn found a pen. Then she sat down on her bed, propping the journal on her lap with a pillow, and began to write. She wrote about Leah's abortion. She wrote what Nathan had told Pastor Russell. She wrote every thought that came into her head. And, she wrote how she felt about everything. She wrote for hours. When finally, her fingers were sore and she was too tired to write anymore, she slid the journal and the pen on the floor under the bed, slipped under the covers, and fell into a deep, dreamless sleep.

A week later in the stables at Redbud, Katelyn walked into Trim Jim's stall to find a much-improved Kiana. The little girl was standing in front of the horse, stroking his nose, chattering away about something that had happened earlier that week. Pat was quiet, tightening the saddle around Trim Jim's ample belly.

"Kiana!" Katelyn exclaimed, touching the girl's shoulder.

Kiana held her finger up to her lips, silencing her while she finished telling her story to her horse. Trim Jim, for his part, held his muzzle down by her face, let her stroke him, and only occasionally shucked out a lungful of air. Katelyn thought it sounded like he was impatient for Kiana to finish, while she could have listened to the cheerful, soft melody of the girl's voice for hours.

"And, then my friends Essie and Spike, I call him that 'cause his hair sticks straight up from his forehead, when we got back after recess, we were late and the teacher, Miss Mack—MacKenzie—was mad. See, I can walk out pretty good, so we'd gone all the way to the far fence. But it's the getting back part that's hard. I get tired and can't catch my breath. Miss Mack said my friends shouldn't have let me go out so far. Essie put her head down on her desk and cried. But Spike looked straight at Miss Mack and said, 'Kiana's got everyone in the world tellin' her 'don't do this, don't do that.' Well, I'm her friend, and I'm just always gonna say, 'You go on and do whatever you feel up to, Kiana. I'm gonna be standing here beside you. I'm gonna carry you home if you need me to.'"

Kiana paused for a moment, her eyes shining. Trim Jim blew out a belly full of air and stomped his foot, eager to get going. Other horses and their riders were filtering by the stall.

"That's what you do, Trim Jim. You carry me home. I get myself here, and then you take me the rest of the way. You're my friend, just like Spike and Essie." Kiana patted him once on the neck, then moved toward his side, where Pat stood waiting to help her mount.

Katelyn watched Kiana closely during the class to see if she could detect any signs of weakness or frailty in this little girl who had come to mean so much to her. But in Kiana's posture, she saw a confident rider, straight-backed with firm hands, knees gripping her mount. Instead of the tiny body on the massive horse, she saw the depth and breadth and height of Kiana's spirit, a spirit that embraced the hopeful optimism that took her out and then accepted with humility the gifts of the others who carried her back when she'd gone beyond her capabilities. That day, Katelyn felt Kiana had surpassed her. She wondered if Mrs. Hurley sometimes felt the same way.

On her way out to her car, Katelyn saw Natalie, the director, waving her over. Natalie was talking to a mother who fiddled with the handle of the car while waiting for Natalie to finish. Two girls waited in the back seat, the smaller one kicking the seat in front of her rhythmically, the older one poised over a book. Katelyn observed them, noticing the similarities between the younger one and her mother, as she waited for Natalie. She wondered whether Leah's baby would have resembled Leah or Carter—and shuddered.

"Katelyn," Natalie said, in greeting, as she turned to her and the car pulled away.

"Yes? What's up?"

"I wondered if you'd given any more thought to where you were going to school and what you were going to study," Natalie said. She said this more as a declaration than as a question, so Katelyn waited for her to continue.

"I was up in Michigan this last week, so I swung by the university to pick this up for you." Natalie reached into her back pocket and pulled out a small brochure, folded several times.

Curious, Katelyn began to unfold the brochure, smoothing it out with her fingers as she did so.

"Sorry for the shape it's in," Natalie said.

"That's okay," Katelyn said, realizing the brochure described a program of study that combined the study of horses with child development and disabilities. Natalie had mentioned the course to her before, encouraging her to consider it. Required courses were heavily weighted toward the sciences, biology, and psychology. She raised her eyebrows and looked back at Natalie.

"It looks interesting," she said. "Thanks."

Natalie nodded. "You're very welcome. When someone has shown such a talent for this work as you have, she deserves encouragement. Have you made any decisions about school?"

"I . . . um. I've applied and been accepted at Marpeck College, where my dad teaches."

"Well, that's a fine place to start. And, you know, for many jobs, especially in such highly specialized fields, it will be your master's degree—as well as your internships—that may more strongly influence your opportunities. As you can see from the brochure, this program offers both a bachelor's and a master's degree in therapeutic horseback riding."

Katelyn took a deep breath. "I haven't thought that far ahead yet."

Natalie looked at her steadily, then said, "No, of course not. You're still quite young. How old are you again, Katelyn?"

"I'll be eighteen next week."

"Well, that's almost an adult, Katelyn. I left home at eighteen. Just promise me you'll think about it. If you have any questions, any at all, just let me know," Natalie said. She smiled. "I forget what it's like to be so young and to have my whole life in front of me—to have so many choices and not to know which path to take."

"To tell you the truth, there's so much going on right now," Katelyn said. "But when things settle down, I'll give it some thought."

When Katelyn returned home, it was nearly one o'clock. The fragrant promise of a hearty meal greeted her.

"Mom? Rachel?" Katelyn called, after stepping out of her shoes and dropping her purse on the floor.

"We're in here," Mom answered from the kitchen. Katelyn heard the sound of her mother's and sister's voices, quieter now, talking to each other as she approached the kitchen. She smiled gratefully.

"Hey, what's going on in here?" she asked, leaning against the doorway.

"We're making tacos," Rachel said, stirring the ground turkey frying in the skillet. Mom stood by the bowls of shredded cheese, chopped tomatoes, black olives, and lettuce.

"You've been busy," Katelyn said. "It smells so good."

Rachel grinned at her. "It was my idea. I thought it would be fun to make lunch with Mom and for the three of us to eat together, for a change." She looked quickly at her mom, and then away, as if she were afraid if she made too much of it, her mom would disappear or change her mind. But Mom, Katelyn thought, did not seem to notice the comment directed at her. She looked happy, following the instructions of her youngest.

"So, how were the kids today?" Mom asked.

"They were great," Katelyn said. "Kiana especially seems to be doing well."

"Is she the one who was in the hospital recently?" Mom asked.

Katelyn was impressed. Her mom had been paying attention after all.

"Oh, Katelyn, before I forget," Rachel said, spooning the ground turkey into a taco shell. "Leah called this morning. She said she'd call you back after lunch."

"Thanks," Katelyn said, realizing she had not talked to Leah for a whole week. She was glad Leah had called. She had thought about her several times, but not found time to call her.

By the time Leah called back, Katelyn and Rachel had washed the dishes. Then Rachel and Mom had disappeared to Rachel's room, leaving Katelyn at the dining room table with her world history book to memorize critical events of the Renaissance Period. Katelyn had set the telephone down on the table and answered it on the first ring.

"Hi. Katelyn?" Leah sounded hesitant.

"Yes. Hi, Leah."

"I had a really great time with you last weekend. I thought you did too."

"I did." Katelyn was confused, but waited.

"You're avoiding me," Leah said quietly.

Katelyn didn't answer. She wasn't sure what to say.

Leah sighed, then asked. "Have you scheduled your appointment with Elaine yet?"

"No, not yet. You said the case might not even go to trial."

"I know. That's what Elaine says. But she says we have to be ready. All of the witnesses have to be ready. You will be ready, just in case, Katelyn, won't you?"

"Yes, of course." Katelyn did not want to see Carter again. Lately, she increasingly blamed him for her problems with Leah. "How will you stand seeing him again?" she asked.

"I think about it every day," Leah said. "I brace myself. I pray for strength and courage. And, I tell myself that once I've done it, I'll never have to think about it again. I'll be free to think about anything else besides Carter and what he's done to me."

There was a long silence. Katelyn could hear Leah biting her nails.

"Well, I gotta go," Leah said finally. "Call me sometime, okay?"

"Okay. Bye." Katelyn knew she should add something, anything that would let Leah know that she supported her. But she couldn't. She remembered the ride to the abortion clinic as clearly as if it were yesterday. Part of her still believed that no matter how badly Carter had treated Leah, no matter what had happened between them, that Leah didn't have the right to make the decision she did. That's what held Katelyn back and stopped her from telling her friend that she was praying too—for Carter to get what he had coming to him, for Leah to be strong and unwavering in her testimony, for God to forgive Leah for having the abortion, and above all, for everything to go back to the way it had been before this whole series of events had messed up all their lives.

After Katelyn hung up the phone, she called Shawn.

"Hey, I was just thinking about you," Shawn said. "What does the word 'renaissance' mean?"

"Shawn. I need a break from studying. Can you come over now?" she jumped in.

He hesitated before answering. "Sure, I can be there in ten minutes."

"Okay. See you soon. Mom and Rachel are here,

but we can go for a walk." Katelyn was about to hang up when she heard him say her name.

"Yeah?" she asked.

"You're not getting ready to dump me, are you? I mean, if you are I might need all those ten minutes to prepare myself."

She was stunned. Was he joking? "No, Shawn, I'm not going to dump you. I just got off the phone with Leah, and I needed someone to talk to." She started closing her books, as if he were already at the door, while she waited for her words to reassure him.

He let out a sigh, and his voice was cheerful. "Great. See you in ten," and he hung up the phone.

Katelyn put the phone down and walked upstairs to Rachel's room. She stood in the doorway a moment, trying not to interrupt. Rachel and Mom were chattering away about a book they had both read, but decided they no longer needed to keep. Finally they stopped and turned to her.

"Mom?" she said. "Shawn's on his way over. We're going out for a walk."

"How is your studying going?" Mom asked.

"Oh, it's coming along. I just need a break."

"Okay," Mom said, arching her eyebrows. Katelyn took this to mean her mother would like to say more, but decided against it.

"So, when the phone rang a few minutes ago . . . was that Leah?" Rachel asked.

"Yes, she called," Katelyn said. "To ask if I'd met with Elaine yet. Mom, will you come with me when I go?"

"I'll try, dear," Mom said. "Depending on when you schedule it. If I can't come, your father will. We've discussed it."

"If you tell me when it will work for you to come with me," Katelyn said, "I'll schedule it then."

"It's just a busy time at work, you know. But sometime after four might work," Mom said. "Then I will leave work a little early, and you won't miss school."

"After four it will be then." Katelyn wanted her mother to come with her. She knew her father would be great, but she needed her mom.

When Shawn arrived a few moments later, Katelyn met him at the door with her shoes and jacket on. He kissed her lightly on the lips.

Katelyn turned and yelled up the stairs, "Shawn's here. We'll be back in an hour."

He grinned at her, holding his hands over his ears. "At least you don't have a dog, too," he said. "Or it could get really noisy in here."

She closed the door behind them, then took his hand as they headed down the stairs.

They walked for a few minutes without speaking.

"It's a beautiful day," Shawn said.

"Is it?" Katelyn asked, looking around her. "Yes, I guess it is." The sun was shining, the breeze was warm and refreshing, and the grass was beginning to turn green.

"What's on your mind, Katelyn?"

She looked at him. What could she tell him? Not much, she thought. Instead, she asked, "You really thought I was going to break up with you?"

Shawn looked away. He kept his eyes on the sidewalk as he said, "Yeah. To tell you the truth, I've been wondering if you liked Leah's brother."

"Noah?" Katelyn was dumbfounded. "Why would you think that?"

"Because ever since he called you a couple of months ago, you've been having problems. You and Leah aren't getting along, you've been losing track of time and showing up late for classes. You have trouble relaxing, and your mind seems to wander a lot."

Katelyn sighed. "I see your point. But I assure you there's nothing between me and Noah. The only reason we've been talking is to figure out how to help

Leah." She chose her words carefully, knowing it would be only too easy to blurt out Leah's secret.

"Are you helping her?" Shawn asked.

"No," she said truthfully. "Not nearly as much as I should be."

"And why is that?"

Katelyn stopped and wrapped her arms around him, glad that his arms immediately surrounded her with their comfort. "I guess because I blame her for this whole situation. I don't understand how she let things go so far with Carter."

"Do you need to know?" Shawn asked, gently stroking her hair.

"Yes," she said. "I guess I do."

"Then maybe you should ask her."

CHAPTER **10**

Katelyn, however, did not find it that easy to just ask Leah about her relationship with Carter. When Leah called the following Thursday afternoon, on Katelyn's birthday, her tone was stiff and business-like.

"I have a present for you, and I'd like to come over and drop it off. Are you going to be home for a little while?"

"Yes, we'll be here. Dad's coming around five to take me and Rachel out for dinner," Katelyn said. "That's not for an hour."

"I won't stay long. I don't want to keep you."

Katelyn didn't know how to respond. Leah sounded angry, but when she arrived, she seemed quiet and uncertain.

"This is for you," she said, handing Katelyn a large flat box, wrapped in beautiful pink and yellow paper, and tied with a yellow ribbon and bow.

"Thank you," Katelyn said.

"You can open it," Leah said, moving across the room to sit on the couch.

Katelyn sat in the armchair across from her, slid the ribbon off the package and lifted off the bow. Then she carefully unwrapped the box. If Leah was impatient, she didn't show it. Her eyes were glued to Katelyn's face as she lifted the lid from the box.

And, she wasn't disappointed.

"Wow! Leah, this is beautiful," Katelyn exclaimed, holding up a green and blue quilted purse. "Did you make it? It's perfect."

Leah nodded and blushed. "Thanks. I got school credit for it, as a project for my home economics unit."

"You did an outstanding job!"

Leah stood up. "I'm glad you like it. Well, I better go."

"You don't have to leave right away," Katelyn said. She didn't want Leah to go.

"No? I mean, yes, I do. Lately, I don't feel very welcome here." Leah breezed past Katelyn and out the door before she could object. But she turned back when she got to her car. "I hope you have a great birthday, Katelyn. Really."

"I'll talk to you soon," Katelyn said. She had made Leah unhappy and she needed to do something about it, she thought as she watched her friend drive away. When she went inside, she looked up Elaine's number in the phone book, and made an appointment for the following Monday at four.

Not long after that, Dad arrived, dressed in a suit and tie.

"She got to you too, I see," Katelyn said, kissing him on the cheek. Rachel had insisted that Katelyn dress up when she got home from school.

The three of them went to an Indian restaurant, one of Katelyn's favorites. When the waiter asked them how many were in their party, Katelyn said, "Three."

"Four," Rachel corrected.

Puzzled, Katelyn turned to her, but Rachel just shook her head. Whoever was coming, Rachel wasn't telling.

The waiter led them to a table. Dad chose a seat against the wall, and Rachel sat across from him. "It's your birthday," she explained. "You get to sit next to Dad tonight."

Katelyn sat down next to Dad, and he quickly put his arm around her, drawing her to him in a quick, half-hug. "Happy birthday, Katydid."

She laughed, pleased he'd used the old nickname.

A moment later, in the dim light of the restaurant, Katelyn watched as a woman approached the table. Suddenly, she panicked—her father's date! Then, as the woman got closer, Katelyn realized it was her mother. Wearing an ivory satin evening gown, with her shoulder-length dark hair pulled back out of her face, Mom didn't look like the woman Katelyn and Rachel lived with. In her arms, Mom carried a large blue and lavender gift box. As she got closer, Katelyn could see her cheeks were slightly pink, as if she were aware that every head in the restaurant had turned to watch her go by.

"Liz, you look amazing," Dad said, standing to greet her. Rachel and Katelyn stood too, unaccustomed to seeing their mother in such splendor.

"Wow, Mom," Rachel said, nodding. "You're hot."

Mom blushed. "Why, thank you, dear." Then she turned to Katelyn and said, "It's all for you, Katie. In honor of your eighteenth birthday."

"Thanks, Mom. You take my breath away," Katelyn said.

As they all sat back down, Rachel chimed in, "It was my idea. I thought you'd like a family party with just the four of us. I helped Mom pick out the dress."

"And, my shirt and tie," Dad said, pulling his tie out so they could all get a good look.

"It's very sharp," Katelyn said, looking it over. "And heaven knows you could always use a new shirt and tie."

They all laughed then, but inside, Katelyn felt soft and tearful. Her family had done this for her. Rachel had asked her father and mother to celebrate her birthday as a family, and they had said yes. No Max, no girlfriend for her father. Just the four of them, out of respect for how they used to be. From time to time during the dinner, Katelyn found herself just looking at each of them, amazed they were talking and joking so easily.

After they had eaten their fill, Mom handed her the gift. Katelyn took the paper off carefully, gently prying loose each piece of tape. When she finally had it unwrapped, she was holding a brand-new laptop computer. "It's incredible," she said, admiring it.

"We knew you'd need it for college," Dad said.

Katelyn smiled at each of them, then felt her face

screw up, fighting tears. Under the table, Rachel kicked her gently.

Katelyn laughed, then let the tears come. "Thanks for the computer. And, for this party. It means a lot," she said. She kicked Rachel back. "And thank you, Rach, for everything you did." She knew Rachel had done it just as much for herself as for Katelyn.

"What did Shawn get you for your birthday?" Dad asked.

"A long-distance phone calling card, so we could keep in touch next year," Katelyn said.

Dad nodded. "Planning ahead."

"A lot can happen in a summer," Mom said.

Katelyn stared at her, then glanced at Rachel, who was also studying their mom. But Mom didn't add anything, and Katelyn soon forgot about it as they stood up to leave.

The next Saturday, Katelyn was disappointed that Kiana did not show up for her class. Natalie stopped by Trim Jim's stall.

"Katelyn, I'm going to have you help out Rex this morning. He's having some trouble settling down. Kiana's mom called and said she's not feeling well, and they won't make class today. But, if you have time, she said Kiana would love it if you could drop by their house in the next few days," Natalie said.

She was in a hurry, it seemed to Katelyn. But there was nothing in her words or her tone that hinted of any crisis.

Still, Katelyn did not wait before arranging a time to see Kiana. That afternoon she asked Shawn to go with her. Shawn, Jason, and Max had come over to help the Neufeld family finish the raking and yard work that hadn't been done very well the previous fall. Jason had brought along his mom's digital camera and was clicking photos of Rachel bagging stray leaves and straggly old vines, Shawn and Katelyn attempting to climb a tree, and Max and Mom pretending to oversee their helpers. They had been working most of the afternoon, and the yard was looking exceptional.

"You think they can spare us here?" he asked, smiling.

"Yeah, I think so," she said, then turned to her mom. "Are we about done here? Is it okay if Shawn and I take off to see Kiana?"

"Sure, honey. I think we're about ready to call it quits anyway."

"I just need to call first," Katelyn said, running inside to call Mrs. Hurley. She returned shortly, motioning Shawn over to the car.

"We're all set," she said. "We should be back in an hour or so."

"Just a sec," Shawn said, and jogged over to Jason. "Can I borrow the camera?"

"You remember how to use it?" Jason handed him the camera.

"Yeah, yeah. I got it." Shawn tucked it into his pocket.

When they got to Kiana's house, Mrs. Hurley met them at the door and greeted them warmly. Katelyn looked beyond her, at the couch where Kiana had been the last time she had visited her. But the couch was empty.

"She's in her room resting," Mrs. Hurley said, noticing Katelyn's gaze. "She's okay, for now. She's had a rough week. Here, it's this way." She led Katelyn and Shawn up the stairs to the second floor.

"Doesn't she have a tough time getting up all these stairs?" Katelyn asked, thinking of how easily Kiana got out of breath.

"I often carry her up. She's as light as a kitten," Mrs. Hurley said. "If we're too tired, we sleep downstairs, but Kiana likes to be in her own room. She's always liked the view from the second floor. She likes being 'almost in the sky,' as she puts it."

Katelyn smiled at Shawn, who smiled back.

"Hey, baby, you have company," Mrs. Hurley said cheerfully to Kiana. The girl was buried so deep in her covers that Katelyn couldn't figure out where she was. But then she stirred, and Mrs. Hurley reached behind her, gently hoisting up the pillows and Kiana along with them.

Kiana stuck both fists in her eyes and gave them a good rubbing.

"Sorry to wake you from the world's most perfect nap," Shawn said, laughing.

She took her fists away from her eyes, grinned a huge grin at him, and patted the bed beside her. Then she turned to Katelyn and grinned at her as well.

"Hey Kiana. How are you?" Katelyn asked, fighting the dread in the pit of her stomach as she tried to reconcile the girl's haunting appearance with her joyful manner. Kiana's eyes appeared large and overly bright, resting on top of dark, sunken half-circles. The bones in her cheekbones and wrists were sharper and more prominent.

Kiana nodded in answer and reached for a deck of cards on the bedside table. She handed them to Shawn.

"Go fish?" he asked.

She nodded again.

"Your hair looks beautiful," Katelyn said. "I love all the yellow beads."

Mrs. Hurley chuckled. "She likes her hair done. I braided it last night. She couldn't sleep, and she wanted to be pretty, in case she felt up to going to church tomorrow."

Kiana put a hand under her ear, posing and batting her eyes. Shawn, seizing the moment, pulled the digital camera out of his pocket and snapped a photo. At first, Kiana looked confused, then she laughed hoarsely.

"Can I take one of you and Katelyn?" Shawn asked. "I thought she would like to have a photo of the two of you. And, maybe you'd like one as well?"

Kiana's eyes glowed. She nodded yes.

Katelyn slipped behind Kiana so her head was almost resting on the pillow, but Kiana turned to look at her. In her eyes Katelyn saw something profound, something she wondered if Shawn could capture with the camera. He snapped a picture, then several more. Then he showed them to Kiana, and she pointed out the ones she liked. He promised to print them out for her and get copies to her.

She whispered, "Soon?"

"Yes. It doesn't take any time at all. I'll print

them out on our color printer when I get home and drop them off at your house."

Kiana clapped her hands. "Today?"

He thought for a moment. "Tomorrow at the latest."

She nodded and leaned back against the pillow, closing her eyes. Shawn picked up the cards and shuffled them, waiting for her to open her eyes.

Katelyn looked at Mrs. Hurley.

"It's okay. She's just resting her eyes. She complains they're dry and itchy. Maybe Shawn, you could come downstairs with me and get a snack. That'll give Katelyn and Kiana a moment."

Kiana opened her eyes and pointed to a box on her dresser. Mrs. Hurley nodded, stood up, and handed it to her daughter. Shawn followed her out of the room.

Katelyn moved around Kiana's legs, trying to get comfortable where Shawn had been sitting.

"Hey sweetie, I missed you at Redbud this morning. And, Trim Jim didn't get his workout either."

Kiana giggled, wrinkling up her nose. She handed the box to Katelyn. "I made this for you," she whispered.

"Why, thank you," Katelyn said, opening the box. Inside was a brown clay horse. "It's beautiful," she said. "And perfect. I will always treasure it." She leaned forward to hug Kiana.

Mrs. Hurley and Shawn came back with cheese, crackers, and apple juice. They played one game of "Go Fish" while eating a snack. Katelyn noticed that although Kiana held a cracker most of the time they were there, she never took a bite and she had only one tiny sip of her apple juice when her mother tilted the glass up to her chin. After the game, Kiana looked very tired so Katelyn and Shawn stood up to leave. When Katelyn leaned over to kiss her cheek, Kiana squeezed her hand, then whispered, "Don't forget. Pictures."

Shawn nodded and held up the camera. "I've got it covered. I'll get your number from Katelyn and give you a call before I come."

"You can leave them inside the storm door," Mrs. Hurley said. "You don't need to call. I expect we'll be home. If you leave them, I'll find them."

Shawn nodded.

At the door, Katelyn gave Mrs. Hurley a hug.

"Thanks for coming, dear. It means a lot to Kiana to have visitors."

"You want to come with me when I bring her the pictures?" Shawn asked, when they were back in the car, strapping on their seatbelts.

"Sure," Katelyn said. "I'm worried about her, Shawn."

Shawn squeezed her hand. "I know. I'm worried about her, too."

Early Sunday evening, Shawn and Katelyn dropped by Kiana's house to deliver the photos. But they found the house dark and quiet. Shawn rang the doorbell, but no one came. Katelyn opened the storm door and leaned the envelope against the wooden door.

"I wonder where they are," Katelyn said.

"Maybe Kiana was feeling better today," Shawn suggested.

She looked at him and smiled. "Thanks for trying to be optimistic. What you really think is?"

"Mrs. Hurley may have had some errands to run and simply taken Kiana with her. It could be nothing more than that."

"I hope you're right." Katelyn reached for his hand. Shawn squeezed her hand, then let go, reaching for something in the back seat. He placed an envelope into her hand.

"I made copies for you, too," he said.

"Thanks," Katelyn said, pressing the envelope against her chest. She was glad to have pictures. The clay horse was sitting next to her bed, so she could see it every morning when she woke up.

That night when Katelyn was going upstairs to bed, she suddenly remembered her appointment with Elaine. She called down to Mom, who was sitting with Max in the living room.

"Mom, you won't forget about tomorrow, will you? You'll meet me at Elaine's office, right?"

"Yes, dear. I've got it. You're dropping Rachel and Hillary off at their dance lesson, first, right?"

"Hillary's mom will pick us up afterwards and take us to her house. When you are done at the lawyer's, one of you can just pick me up on your way home," Rachel said.

"I'll plan on it," Mom offered. Satisfied, Rachel went up to her room.

"Mom?" Katelyn asked, lingering.

"What is it?"

"Will you come tuck me in?"

"Sure," Mom said, standing up and following her.

"Me too," Rachel yelled.

"Yes, you too," Mom called, going to Katelyn's room first.

Katelyn climbed into bed, then looked at her mom.

"What is it, honey?" Mom asked, sitting on the bed.

"I'm scared I'll have to testify in Carter's case and that I won't be able to."

"Why wouldn't you be able to?"

"I don't know. Like when people know they should move out of the path of an oncoming car, and they freeze."

"You won't freeze, Katelyn. The lawyer tomorrow will talk to you about the case and help you rehearse what you'll say, so you'll be more comfortable."

"But Carter won't be there."

"No, he won't. That's true. But think how much harder it will be for Leah, Katie."

"I do, Mom. How can she stand it?"

"I don't know. She's been through a lot."

Katelyn thought her mother didn't know the half of it. But her mother wasn't finished. She added, "She's an amazing person, your friend, Leah. I think she's one of the strongest young women I know." She got up to leave.

"Mom?"

"Yes?"

"Could you kiss me goodnight?"

"Sure, dear." She kissed Katelyn softly on her cheek. "It'll be fine, Katelyn. You'll do great."

Monday afternoon when Katelyn arrived at the lawyer's office, she was surprised to find her mom leafing through a magazine, waiting for her. She stood up when she saw Katelyn and glanced at the receptionist, who said, "I'll take you back. Elaine will just be a moment."

Katelyn and her mother followed the receptionist down a hall and into a conference room. "Can I get you a cup of coffee or a cola?" she asked before leaving.

"I'd love a cup of coffee. Black's fine," Mom said. "Katelyn?"

"Yeah, I'll have a cola." Her mouth was dry.

The receptionist came back and set a mug in front of Mom and a glass with cola and ice in front of Katelyn. Elaine breezed in only a moment later, warmly shaking hands as she introduced herself. Then she went over a few instructions before beginning the questions.

"Katelyn, can you tell me about the incident when you met Leah at the drugstore in December?"

"She called and asked me to come get her. I . . . my mom and Shawn came along with me. We picked her up and drove her to the hospital."

"Why did you take her there instead of home?"

Katelyn stared at her. "She was bleeding from her stomach."

"Any other visible signs that she needed medical care?" Elaine asked, taking notes.

"Her forehead was beginning to show signs of bruising," Mom added. "Her lip was also bleeding."

"She showed me her stomach later, at the hospital, where Carter had used the knife," Katelyn found she could not say he had cut Leah.

"You've known Leah for quite some time," Elaine said. "Is that correct?"

Katelyn nodded.

"Have you ever known her to hurt herself?"

"What do you mean?"

"Is it possible she would have carved the word into her stomach to make it appear Carter had done it?" Elaine asked.

"No." Carter had carved the word "MINE" into Leah's flesh. Katelyn knew Leah would never have done that.

Elaine accepted this. "What did Leah say had happened?"

"She said Carter had beaten her up."

"Nothing else?"

"No."

Elaine scribbled a few notes, then looked up.

"Tell me what happened the night of your sister's ballet performance."

Katelyn took a sip from her glass and then told her how after the performance, Carter had been hiding behind a drinking fountain, waiting for them in the crowded hallway. He had tripped Leah, and then pulled her up and backed away. She had reached for Leah, wanting to pull her back, but Carter had cut her arm with the knife he had hidden until then. She described how Carter had turned the knife on Leah first, saying he only wanted to talk to her. When Katelyn saw Shawn had a chance to help, she had tried to distract Carter.

"What happened next?" Elaine asked.

Katelyn paused. She didn't want to talk about the fight between Carter and Shawn.

"It's okay, honey," Mom said. "Shawn will be okay."

"Shawn threw his bowling ball at him. He hadn't wanted to leave it in the car, so he'd brought it in. Carter saw it at the last minute and tried to catch it, but he fell and dropped the knife. Leah got the knife, and Shawn jumped on Carter and . . . was fighting with him."

Elaine asked a few more questions and leaned back in her chair. "I presume Leah's told you that we don't expect this case to go to trial," she said, tapping her pencil against her hand.

"Yes, she mentioned that," Katelyn said.

"I expect his legal counsel to try to plea bargain since he may not have much of a chance in court. There is such a strong case against Carter," Elaine said, addressing Katelyn's mother. "We've got two separate incidents of his violent behavior against Leah. Both are well-documented. In the first case, we have the records from the hospital and in the second, we have a number of eye witnesses. The charges against him are serious and include assault and battery, rape, assault with a deadly weapon. . . ."

But Katelyn was having trouble listening. "Rape?" she asked, feeling the color drain from her face as she turned to her mother. "Carter raped Leah?"

Mom nodded and reached for her hand. "Yes. Your father and I, we thought you knew. The day the charges were noted in the newspaper, he called me."

"Why didn't you tell me?" Katelyn asked, shaking her head.

"You and Leah are such good friends, Katie. We thought Leah would have told you."

"No," Katelyn said, looking away from her mother and back at Elaine. "She didn't tell me. I never knew."

CHAPTER 11

Walking out to their cars after the appointment with Elaine, Katelyn told her mom she was going to stop by Leah's before she went home.

"Don't be too hard on her," Mom said, turning to unlock her car.

"What do you mean?" Katelyn asked, frowning.

"Just what I said. You look upset. Maybe you should wait until you calm down before talking to her."

Katelyn considered her words carefully before speaking. "Waiting a few hours or days won't change things."

"It might change the way you're feeling."

"I'll be home in a couple of hours," Katelyn said, yanking open the car door and plopping down behind the wheel.

From her car, Mom nodded at her and pulled out. Katelyn could see her mother disapproved of what she was doing, but she had to talk to Leah. It couldn't wait. She knew her feelings would only get worse if she waited, and she thought they were as bad as they could get.

But when she got to Leah's and looked in the rear-view mirror at her tear-streaked face, Katelyn stopped to wonder if she should have listened to her mother after all. She realized that she'd been crying the whole drive over from the lawyer's, and she hadn't even been aware of it. She wiped her face with some tissues, then got out of the car and walked up to the house. She was at Leah's house now. Even if her mother had been right, even if she should have waited, she would not turn back.

Katelyn hesitated on the doorstep listening to the sounds of the family's voices around the dining room table. They sounded so normal, she thought—the twins' cheerful bantering, the melodic exchange of Pete's deeper, masculine voice with Ginger's softer, even voice. Leah occasionally added something, her expressive voice resonating up and down the scale, even in the few words she contributed.

Katelyn rang the bell. The talking stopped for a moment. She heard a child's footsteps running toward the door and wasn't surprised to see Jonah's wide grin as he pulled open the door.

Immediately, though, his grin faded. "Katelyn. Hi, come in," he said. "I'll get Leah."

Stepping inside, Katelyn realized he'd gone before she could return his greeting. Her face must have appeared very grim to him if he hadn't lingered to tease her.

A moment later, Leah stood in the entranceway. She came in quietly and with a dignity that made Katelyn's breath catch in her throat. She wanted to reach for her friend—to have her friend hold her through this terrible time. She wanted to console her for what Carter had done, but that had already been a long time ago, she thought, and she'd already failed Leah by not being a friend Leah had been able to confide in, and for not having been able to imagine the worst and offer comfort before it had been requested.

"I met with Elaine today," Katelyn said. Her words came out a croak.

Leah nodded, then slipped her arm in Katelyn's and led her upstairs.

"Why didn't you tell me?" Katelyn asked, as soon as Leah had closed the door.

Leah sat down in the armchair and looked up at her, studying her. "You mean about the rape charges?"

"Yes. Exactly." Katelyn was standing, still wearing her jacket, as if Leah could tell her in just a few moments what she had been living with for months.

"I was ashamed, I guess, at first. Embarrassed." Leah looked down at her hands.

"But Leah, it wasn't your fault," Katelyn said, sinking down onto her friend's bed.

Leah looked directly at Katelyn. "Yeah," she said.

Katelyn waited, wanting her to go on, trying to keep hold of her friend by maintaining eye contact, to keep Leah from looking away or even more importantly, retreating into herself when Katelyn was finally beginning to understand.

"You know how we've grown up together, and all these things we've done—sleeping at each other's houses, swimming at the pool in the summer, playing chess," Leah stopped.

Katelyn nodded.

"All these things, they bring us close and somehow these things we do and how we feel about doing them are what make us friends, right?"

Katelyn nodded again.

"Well," Leah said. "When you and Nathan got interested in each other, you tried to share that experience with me by telling me about it. And, I appreciated it. But I still wanted something like it for myself. But what happened with Carter—and not just the rape—but so much of the relationship—was a wedge between you and me. I couldn't tell you some of it, like when we began to have sex. And, I couldn't tell you about his jealousy, because you wouldn't have understood him . . ."

"But . . ." Katelyn tried to interrupt.

Leah smiled. "No, I know you. You would have told me to get out of the relationship—I know it because I would have told you the same thing. You could tell me everything about Nathan because there was no dark side to the relationship."

"That's not true," Katelyn said. "I mean, I think there is a dark side to it."

"Maybe now, looking back. Maybe there were some things that happened that weren't ideal or that you could have learned from. But the fact is we both know that Nathan is a decent guy who really cared about you and was trying to have a good relationship with you."

"And, what was Carter?" Katelyn asked, trying to keep up with where Leah was going.

Leah nodded and smiled again, picking at her jeans. "Carter was, Carter is a very troubled young man who wanted to have someone in the world he could call his own—completely and utterly. And, he was persistent. He would stop at nothing to get it." She waited.

"Tell me what happened," Katelyn said, her voice pleading. She knew she was really asking Leah to trust her.

"That day, when I called you from the drugstore, Carter got jealous about a waiter who served us ice cream," Leah said. "We were supposed to go Christmas shopping, but Carter was too angry and insisted we go back to his apartment. Once we got there, he wouldn't talk to me at first. I tried to make up with him, to reassure him that everything was fine and that I loved only him. But I wasn't very convincing, because I'd already realized I wanted to end the relationship. Finally, though, he relaxed and we started to make love."

Katelyn felt her eyes get big.

Leah almost laughed, but stopped herself. "It was

Carter who got up to get a condom. He was trying to show me he wanted to protect me from getting pregnant. But he was gone just a moment too long so I went to check on him. When I found him in the bathroom, he was using a safety pin to make a hole in the condom.

"I was furious," Leah said, her voice a little louder. "I guessed this was not the first time he had messed with a condom, and I started screaming at him. He was angry I had caught him in the act. He knocked me down several times as I tried to get away from him. When I got back to the living room, I fell against the coffee table. Then he forced himself on me."

The girls were quiet for a few minutes, alone in their thoughts.

"He kept saying I belonged to him. That he loved me and I was his," Leah said, her voice flat and hard. "He tried to get me to agree with him, but I wouldn't. Then, when he'd finished, he got the knife and wrote on my stomach."

Katelyn suddenly realized what the word "MINE" that Carter had carved into Leah's flesh had meant. "So he meant you and any . . . baby were his?"

Her friend nodded.

"So that's why you wanted to have the abortion?

Because you were raped?" To Katelyn, this finally made sense. She stood up, ready to cross the room to be closer to Leah.

But Leah's eyes had narrowed and warned her to keep her distance.

Katelyn was confused and asked, "Why didn't you just tell me?"

"It's very simple," Leah said, leaning back in her seat. "First of all, I can't be sure if I got pregnant the time he raped me or the other times when I chose to have sex with him—especially since he may have tampered with the condoms before."

"But I can see why it would have been harder . . ." Katelyn started, but Leah interrupted.

"It shouldn't matter to you why I wanted an abortion. You were my best friend, Katelyn. You, of all people, should have trusted me and accepted whatever decision I made."

"But . . ." Katelyn felt a stab in her chest and the tears form in her eyes. They were still best friends, weren't they?

"No," Leah said, standing up.

"I'm sorry." The words came out a whisper.

"It's too late for that," Leah said. "I don't want to see you again. I want you to go home now."

"I can't," Katelyn wailed. "I love you."

"I don't want to hear it. Go home." Leah was resolute, her voice even, and her eyes clear.

"No, please, Leah. Please give me another chance. Please don't send me home." Katelyn was crying hard now, speaking between sobs. She couldn't bear to lose Leah's friendship.

There was a quiet knock on the door.

"Yes?" Leah asked.

"I was just checking. Is everything all right in there?" Pete asked.

Leah went to the door and opened it so he could see her face. "Yes," she said. "I'm fine, Daddy. Katelyn's upset and needs to leave now. Would you show her out?"

Without a word, Katelyn breezed past Leah and her father, down the steps, and out of the house. She sat sobbing in her car for a while, afraid to leave, afraid she would never be invited back.

Finally, Katelyn turned the key in the ignition and drove slowly away from Leah and toward home. When she got there, she found Mom, Max, and Rachel in the living room.

"How did it go?" Mom asked, then saw her face and shook her head sadly. In that split second, Katelyn understood her mother was not saying "I told you so," but was grieving with her.

Katelyn turned to go upstairs.

"Katelyn?" Rachel said, behind her.

"It's okay, Rach. I just need to be alone tonight," Katelyn said, continuing up the stairs. She went into her bedroom, took off her jacket, lay down on her bed, and cried herself to sleep.

The next morning, when she awoke, she felt empty and drained. Her head throbbed and the light hurt her eyes. She took a slow shower, dressed mechanically, and joined her family at the breakfast table.

Rachel reached over and squeezed her hand. Katelyn got tears in her eyes.

"How are you doing, Katelyn?" Mom asked.

"I have a headache," she said.

"I don't want you to take any aspirin today, dear," she said. "I'd like you to take that prescription that worked so well the last time."

Katelyn nodded.

"But you can't take it on an empty stomach. And, you didn't have any supper last night. Can you eat something this morning?" Mom asked.

"I'll try."

Mom went to get the medicine, while Rachel jumped up. "I'll get you something to eat," she said.

"Thanks," Katelyn said.

On her way past, Rachel slipped her arm around Katelyn's shoulder and squeezed it.

Katelyn closed her eyes and listened to the sounds of her mother and sister moving around the house. Rachel returned first and set a bowl of cereal in front of her, along with a glass of orange juice.

"Umm," Katelyn said, after her first bite. By the time Mom came back, she had eaten a few more bites.

Mom handed her the pill, and Katelyn washed it down with juice.

"After you're done eating, I want you to lie down for a few minutes and relax so the medicine can take effect. You might be a little late for school, but I want to be sure you're well enough to go before I leave. If I drop you girls off on my way to work, then maybe you could get Shawn and Jason to give you a ride home?"

"Yes!" Rachel said eagerly.

Mom smiled tenderly at her. "You like him, don't you?"

Rachel grinned.

Katelyn ate a few more bites, got up from the table, and took her plate to the kitchen. She went upstairs, brushed her teeth, then went downstairs and stretched out on the living room couch. Within moments, she was so relaxed, she was almost dreaming. By the time her mother called her, her headache was almost gone.

At school, Katelyn sat quietly in her classes, trying to listen, trying not to remember her conversation with Leah. Shawn found her at lunch and sat down with her.

"What's the matter?" he asked.

"I . . ." she shook her head. "I can't talk about it right now."

"Can't or won't?" he asked gently.

"Will you drive me and Rachel home tonight? She'd like it if Jason could come too. We can talk about it then. If I tell you now," she said, moving her food around on her tray, "I'll start crying, and I won't be able to get through the day."

Shawn's eyes filled with concern.

Katelyn waited. "Well, will you?"

"Of course. I'm here for you—to drive you wherever your heart desires to go," he paused to grin at her, "And to listen whenever you want to tell me what's going on."

The rest of the day passed slowly for Katelyn. She listened to the drone of her teachers' voices, doodled in her notebooks, and watched the clock. When her last class was finally released, she went straight to her locker, dumped her textbooks in it, and made her way through the crowded hall to Shawn's locker. While she waited for him, she watched her fellow students and wondered what burdens they each carried. Some of the girls, she reflected, had probably experienced what Leah had—had dated someone who was abusive, or had been raped, or had even had an abortion. Some of these other students—her age or younger—had known the kind of loss Katelyn was feeling—the loss of someone they loved: a friend, a parent, or a sibling. Somehow, despite the burdens collectively borne by the student body of one high school in Northern Indiana, the building could barely contain the life that pulsed through its halls. These were the thoughts Shawn interrupted when Katelyn spotted him moving quickly and gracefully through the crowd as if it were a basketball court.

"Hey," he said, slipping his arm around her waist and pulling her toward him in a quick embrace. "Sorry it was such a rough day."

"It just got a little better," Katelyn said, trying to smile.

"Aww."

They met up with Jason and Rachel and drove home. Katelyn let the others do most of the talking. When they walked in the door, Rachel pulled Jason off to Mom's study to show him something she had found on the Internet. Katelyn was glad to be alone with Shawn. But no sooner had she sat down, or rather sprawled out all over the couch, than the phone rang.

"I'll get it," Shawn said. He picked up the phone and said, "Neufeld residence."

Katelyn shook her head in amazement.

"Yes, yes, she's right here. We just walked in the door. I'll give her the phone," he said, handing the phone to Katelyn. "It's your mom wondering about your headache."

"You're such a great personal assistant," she said. Then, "Hi, Mom."

"Hi, Katelyn. How are you feeling, dear?"

"Better. The medicine is still working."

"I'll be home around five-thirty. I'll pick up supper on the way. Do you think Shawn would be willing to stay with you until I get there?"

Katelyn laughed. "Shawn, will you stay here and babysit me until my mom gets home?"

He nodded and gave her a thumbs-up.

"Yes, Mom. He'll stay."

"Good. I'll see you soon."

"Mom?"

"Yes, Katelyn?"

"Thanks for calling to check on me."

"Of course. I was worried about you. By the way, your father's also concerned. He'd like to come over tomorrow afternoon and spend some time with you while Rachel's at dance class."

"Okay. Bye."

Katelyn ended the call and turned to Shawn, who sat down opposite her on the couch, pulled off her shoes, and began to massage her feet.

"That feels good," she said, setting down the phone.

He smiled.

"Leah doesn't want to be friends anymore," Katelyn said, jumping in to get it over with. "I saw her yesterday, and I finally felt like I understood something important that was going on in her life, and she got angry and sent me home." She felt the emptiness come back and her stomach began to hurt. How could she stand to lose Leah?

"So, she's angry. Maybe she didn't mean it to be quite so final," he suggested.

Katelyn shook her head no. "She meant it. She never wants to see me again."

"Jeez, that's harsh." He looked at her, and his eyes were filled with compassion.

Katelyn pulled her foot away and threw her arms around his neck. She let herself cry the tears she had been holding back all day. Shawn held her, stroking her back and hair, occasionally saying soothing words.

When she began to quiet down, Shawn said, "I know it seems hopeless now. But you and Leah have been friends for years, right?"

"Yeah."

"So maybe it's too soon to just give up. Sometimes we need to fight for the people we love."

"Fight? How?" Katelyn was confused.

"I mean, you have to hang on to your hope that there can be a way back to your friendship. Maybe that means accepting she doesn't want to talk to you right now. But maybe it means she still needs to know you care about her."

"I . . . but I'm the one who needs to know she cares about me!"

Shawn chuckled.

"What's funny?" Katelyn was too tired to be offended.

"You just sounded like a little kid. I know," he squeezed her arm. "I know you want to know she cares about you. But she may also need your reassurance. If you accept her sending you away without a protest, then couldn't she wonder how important she was to you to begin with?"

"Oh, I don't know." She was exasperated and felt contrary. "Or she could conclude I wasn't respecting her decision and that I was stalking her like Carter."

"Yes, you're right," Shawn said, calm. "There's a balance in there somewhere, between just letting it go and hanging on for dear life."

Katelyn didn't answer, but she was listening.

"I trust you will find it," he said.

Over the next few days, Katelyn wrestled with herself, trying to decide whether to call Leah. She spent a lot of time crying alone in her room at first. But Rachel put a stop to that. When Mom told Rachel why Katelyn was so upset, Rachel refused to let her sister be alone. If Katelyn wouldn't come downstairs, Rachel took the cards and cribbage board up to her sister's room and dealt her a hand. If Katelyn wouldn't play, Rachel played solitaire and talked her ear off about anything—and it seemed to Katelyn, everything—that had happened at school that day. Katelyn suspected that Rachel had an opinion about the rift between Leah and herself, and that she probably blamed Katelyn for it, but, to her credit, Rachel did not broach the subject.

The only time Katelyn could honestly say she wasn't thinking about Leah that first week was when she drove into the parking lot of Redbud Saturday morning and saw Mrs. Hurley's beat-up station wagon. She practically ran to Trim Jim's stall, eager to see Kiana. She found the little girl brushing her horse's front leg, murmuring quiet words.

"You're late," Pat said, clearly disappointed.

"Am I?" Katelyn said, looking at her watch. Not that late, she thought. Only ten minutes. "Sorry." Then to Kiana, "It's so good to see you!"

Kiana turned to face her, giving her a small warm smile. "I got the pictures. Thanks."

"You're very welcome." Katelyn scrutinized Kiana's face. She still looked tired, but today she looked determined.

During the class, Kiana seemed just a step behind the other students, but she was trying so hard, Katelyn hardly noticed. She didn't realize the effort it was taking Kiana until after the class when the girl turned to her.

"Carry me?" she asked.

Katelyn scooped her up without a word and carried Kiana to her car. Mrs. Hurley was standing there, waiting for them. She took Kiana from Katelyn, and set her down in the car seat. Kiana motioned for Katelyn to come closer, and kissed her on the cheek while her mom got into the car.

Katelyn closed the door and stood there waving until the car passed out of view.

That afternoon, when Katelyn got home, she wrote Leah a short note.

Leah, I'm so sorry I let you down. I know you don't want to see me now, and I respect your wishes. I just want you to know that I love you. I will always love you. And, I have to hold on to the hope that someday we'll be friends again because I can't imagine my life without you.
—Katelyn

When she finished the note, Katelyn drove over to the Grahams' house and left in in their mailbox. She found it comforting to be so close to Leah, even if she couldn't go up to the door and knock.

CHAPTER **12**

Early one Friday evening a few weeks later, Katelyn, Rachel, and Dad were sitting around his kitchen table. Katelyn had her books spread out and was trying to study. It was past the middle of May, and with finals fast approaching, Katelyn was realizing that her grades were about to take a hit. This last month she had missed classes because of more frequent headaches and had trouble concentrating when she was there. She was behind on the assignments for many of her classes. Her chemistry teacher, the least sympathetic in Katelyn's mind, had given her the weekend to turn in the past four assignments or take a zero on them.

When Dad had picked up the girls around four, he asked about homework, and kept asking until Katelyn had told him everything she had due. Rachel's eyes had opened wide, but Dad had said simply, "Well, I guess we'll make it a homework weekend."

So the three sat around the table: Dad reading the newspaper, Rachel reading a novel assigned by her English teacher, and Katelyn trying to finish her first assignment for her chemistry class before they ate supper. She had just written the answer to the last question on the study sheet when her father said, "Well, what do you know?"

Both girls looked up. He passed the newspaper to Katelyn, his finger tapping an item under a section called "Court News."

Katelyn read the paragraph and, stunned, looked at her father.

"What is it?" Rachel asked.

"Leah's boyfriend, Carter," Dad said. "Has taken a plea bargain for the charges against him and is going to jail for twenty-five years."

"Twenty-five years!" Rachel exclaimed.

"Well, the sentence is twenty-five years," Dad

said. "But he could be out in half of that easily, what with prison overcrowding, and depending on what kind of prisoner he is while behind bars."

A picture came to Katelyn's mind of Carter behind bars. Of course, he had been in the county courthouse for a couple of months already, but she had not imagined what that was like. Now that she did imagine it, she didn't like it.

"It must be awful," she said, shuddering. "To be locked up day after day in a room with three or four or five other prisoners . . ."

Dad looked at her. "Yes, Katelyn. From what I understand, it's pretty rough on a man. But Carter is a young man who committed some very serious crimes against Leah, and he has proven he cannot be trusted with his freedom right now."

"Are you going to call Leah?" Rachel asked.

"I'd like to," Katelyn said. Would Leah talk to her?

"C'mon," Dad said to Rachel. "Let's get out of here and give your sister some privacy." He stood up and went into the living room. Rachel crossed her fingers, then nodded at her sister before following Dad.

Katelyn picked up the receiver and punched in Leah's number. The phone rang several times, then she heard Pete's recorded voice say, "You've reached the Graham residence. If you have a message for one of us, please leave it at the tone."

After the tone, Katelyn said, "Hi, it's Katelyn calling. Leah, I saw the notice in the paper today about Carter. I wanted to let you know I'm thinking about you. I hope you're doing okay." She couldn't ask Leah to call her. She couldn't assume Leah wanted to be her friend.

Katelyn hung up the phone and joined Dad and Rachel in the living room. "She wasn't there, but I left her a message."

Rachel reached out to take her hand.

"Are you about finished with that first assignment?" Dad asked.

"Yes. I had just finished when you handed me the paper," Katelyn said.

"Well, then. Let's go get some supper, and then get back here so you can get some more work done tonight," he said. "There's an old science fiction thriller on at eleven. If you can get a couple more assignments done before that, we'll all get to stay up and watch the movie."

"And if not?" Katelyn asked, finding her father's enthusiasm amusing.

"Hey, I'm all about the rewards," he said. "I don't

even consider the punishments this early in the evening. But I hear some people can only comprehend complex chemistry principles early in the morning—at five o'clock, or something like that."

"Yeah, right," muttered Rachel affectionately. "Like he could give up his time alone in the morning to make you do chemistry."

"Being a parent requires sacrifices," Dad laughed. "If I've told you once, I've told you a thousand times."

"Yes, you have," Katelyn said. "Now let's get going so I can tackle the next assignment."

By Saturday evening, Dad's disciplined approach to Katelyn's schoolwork had yielded results. She had caught up in her algebra, chemistry, and world history classes before he dropped the girls off at home.

As soon as Katelyn got in the door, she called Shawn.

"What are you doing tomorrow afternoon?" she asked.

"Studying for exams. You?"

"I need to study too. Will you come over and study with me?"

"Only if you get something done. Lately, studying with you is like studying with a zombie," Shawn said, good-naturedly. "Watching you not concentrating is distracting."

"I got lots done at Dad's," Katelyn said, telling him of her achievements.

"That's impressive," Shawn said. "But don't forget about the one-page response paper to the Alice Walker short story that's due Monday."

"Oh yeah, thanks for the reminder. I was going to read it tomorrow morning before church. Shawn?"

"Yeah?"

"Did you hear about Carter?"

"Yes. Elaine called Friday to let us know that Carter was going to jail. Part of his deal included not pressing charges against me for that fight," he said.

"So you don't have to go to counseling anymore?"

"No, I guess not. But my mom wants me to keep it up a little longer. She thinks I'm getting something out of it."

The two talked for a few more minutes, then Katelyn had to go get another assignment done before she went to bed. Her father had scheduled all her homework out so she could catch up by the end of the week. She appreciated his help. Somehow, this way, it was easier for her to concentrate, knowing someone else had tracked all her work and was holding her to the task of completing it.

When she crawled into bed Saturday night, she was exhausted, but satisfied she had done her best. She lay there quietly with her eyes open for a few minutes, saying a prayer for Leah and one for Carter. Then she drifted off to sleep.

At the beginning of the week, Katelyn was able to concentrate better than she had been in weeks.

"We'll have to have more 'homework only' weekends," she joked with her dad, when she called him at his office Wednesday afternoon. Rachel was at her dance class, and Mom was still at work.

He laughed. "College is just around the corner. You may as well get used to them now."

"Thanks, Dad, for helping me feel like I could do it," Katelyn said.

"You can do it."

"I have done it. But you know what I mean. It seemed too much before."

"That's okay, Katie. Everyone gets overwhelmed sometimes. Hey, I need to run. I've got a student at my door and a class in a half hour. See you tomorrow."

Katelyn was smiling when she put down the phone. She went to the kitchen, poured herself a glass of milk, and got a granola bar from the cupboard. Then she plopped down on the couch with the remote control to watch a few minutes of television before getting back to her schoolwork. But, before she could turn on the television, the phone rang. She jumped up and grabbed the receiver off the dining room table where she had left it.

"Hello?" she said, trying to finish the bite of granola bar so she could speak more clearly.

"Hello. Is this Katelyn?"

"Yes, it's me," she said.

"Katelyn, it's Mrs. Hurley, Kiana's mom," she said.

Katelyn felt a pang, realizing she hadn't thought about Kiana for days. "Hi, Mrs. Hurley. How is Kiana doing?"

There was a pause.

Then Mrs. Hurley said, "Well, dear, that's why I'm calling. Kiana passed on in her sleep last night."

"I'm sorry. What did you say?" Katelyn asked, sitting down hard on the dining room chair. She must have misunderstood.

"Kiana wanted me to call you. She didn't want you to hear it from Natalie," Mrs. Hurley spoke gently. "She always enjoyed her horseback riding lessons with you."

"I just can't believe it," Katelyn said. "I can't believe she's gone."

"She's in a better place, dear. She suffered so much. There is no suffering where she is now."

The two were silent for a few moments. Katelyn realized Mrs. Hurley was waiting for her to speak.

"And, how are you doing?" Katelyn asked, knowing the loss to Kiana's mother must be more devastating than for anyone else.

"I . . ." Mrs. Hurley trailed off. "I . . . miss her dreadfully." Her voice broke. "The house is so quiet," she continued speaking through her tears. "I keep feeling I need to go get her, to bring her home—as if she is just in the hospital or at school."

Katelyn felt her eyes fill with tears. "She was a great kid."

"Yes, she was." Mrs. Hurley sniffed once, then chuckled. "She made me promise not to be crying all the time, that girl. She made me promise to remember the good times. That's what we're going to do, Katelyn. You come to the celebration of her life. Kiana always said she wasn't having a funeral. She loved drawing, you know. So, we—her grandma and I—thought it would be nice at Kiana's celebration for everyone to draw a picture of something that reminded them of her. Then we'll share the pictures and our memories of her. It will be a week from today at Redbud in the afternoon. Natalie said we could have the meeting there. I thought Kiana would like that."

"I'll be there—with Shawn if that's okay," she said, then thought of something. "Oh, and Mrs. Hurley?"

"Yes?"

"Could you bring the deck of cards? The 'Go Fish' cards? If you don't have a use for them, it would mean a lot to me to have them."

"Yes, Katelyn. I'd be glad for you to have them."

When she hung up the phone, Katelyn was stunned. She felt the familiar ache of loss beginning in her chest. How could she lose both Leah and Kiana in such a short time? She didn't feel she could bear it. She needed a friend, her best friend. This time she had to talk to Leah, she thought as she dialed the Graham residence.

Jonah answered the phone. "Hi, Katelyn, how are you?" he said, warmly.

"Jonah, I need to talk to Leah."

"I'm not sure she'll come to the phone for you," he said, uncertainly. "I can ask her, but I'm afraid she'll say no."

Katelyn thought for a minute. "Tell her that Kiana died and I need her."

He left the phone and returned again a moment later, breathless. "She said . . ."

Katelyn felt a moment of panic. Why hadn't Leah come to the phone?

". . . You could come over. She'll see you in a few minutes and . . ."

"What?" Katelyn asked, impatiently.

"Drive carefully," Jonah said.

Katelyn didn't even say goodbye. She hung up, scratched a note to her mom, and grabbed her purse and keys. She drove as carefully as she could, tears streaming down her cheeks—alternately sad for Kiana, and grateful for Leah. She drove as slowly as she could stand to, with her heart racing toward Leah.

When she got to the Graham residence, she parked the car, and ran up the sidewalk. The door opened before she rang the bell. Leah pulled her in and enfolded Katelyn in her arms.

Katelyn held on tight, letting the tears come. When she realized Leah was crying too, that only made her cry harder.

After a short while, Katelyn felt a nudge at her side. She turned to see Jonah standing there, holding out a box of tissues. He looked down and mumbled something about them needing to pull themselves together.

"Thanks, sweetie," Leah said, taking the box and tousling her brother's hair. "We'll be fine. Just give us a few minutes." Jonah turned, glancing back once, before heading into the kitchen.

"He hates to see people cry," Leah whispered to Katelyn, as she maneuvered her up the stairs. "He's so empathetic, it makes him want to cry, too."

"Must run in your family," Katelyn offered.

"Something like that. I'm just so glad to see you. And," Leah waited until Katelyn was facing her, "I'm so sorry I sent you away." Leah's eyes filled with new tears.

"It's okay," Katelyn said. "I mean, it's okay now."

They sat down on the bed, side-by-side, both leaning against the headboard with their legs stretched out in front of them.

"Tell me about Kiana," Leah said.

"First, tell me about Carter. How are you feeling about everything now?"

Leah reflected. "It's a huge relief to have it all over with. I feel safer, and I know my parents feel I'm safer. At the same time, I feel terribly sorry for Carter. I wish he could be well. You know, that he could get better. I feel so responsible for sending him to prison, but I don't have the reassurance that he'll learn anything from being there."

Katelyn reached for Leah's hand. "That's got to be hard."

Her friend smiled at her. "Thanks."

"For what?"

"For not telling me he got what he deserved."

"Oh that. I didn't think that would make you feel better."

Leah nodded, and put her head against Katelyn's shoulder. "So, tell me about Kiana, your little horseback riding friend."

"I think she knew she was going to die."

"Well, of course she did. Kids who live with long-term illnesses often know."

"No. I mean, I think she knew she was going to die soon. She gave me a gift recently so I wouldn't forget her. It was a brown clay horse she had made. I hate it that she died so young. There was so much of life she never got to experience."

"Maybe," Leah said. "But maybe she learned early how to really appreciate what she had because she knew she wouldn't be here long enough to take any of it for granted."

The two young women sat together talking, oblivious to time. Finally, Ginger called to them.

"Leah, would you like to have Katelyn stay for supper? We'll be eating in about five minutes."

Katelyn stood up quickly. "No thanks, Ginger. I've got a lot of studying to do, and I need to get home."

"You're welcome to stay," Ginger said, opening the door and smiling. "You'll have to eat somewhere."

"She's right, of course," Leah said, standing up.

"Can I take a raincheck? I'd love to have dinner with you when I can relax and not worry about the time."

"Yeah, why don't you join us for supper after your exams are over?" Leah said. "Noah should be home by then." Leah winked at Katelyn, who just grinned back at her.

"Jonah doesn't need any competition from his big brother," Katelyn said. "That would hardly be fair." If Katelyn were truthful, she was looking forward to seeing Noah. Her opinion of him had changed over these last few months.

At the door, Katelyn gave Leah another hug. "I'll call you tomorrow," she said.

Leah nodded, her eyes bright with love. "If I don't call you first."

When she got home, Mom, Max, and Rachel

were eating supper at the dining room table. Rachel jumped up to greet her. "So, tell us, what happened," she prodded eagerly.

"She saw your note," Mom said.

Katelyn smiled. "Leah and I are friends again."

"Yippee!" Rachel yelled at the top of her lungs.

"I'm so glad, Katelyn," Mom said, warmly.

"Yes, it is great. But now I have to eat fast and get some homework done. Is there any food left?" Katelyn picked up the empty plate they had set for her. There would be time later to tell them about Kiana. She wanted to tell Shawn first.

"There's enough," Max said. "And there's more in the kitchen."

Mom smiled at him. "Max brought over dinner tonight, Katelyn. Enough lasagna to feed twenty people."

"Sounds good to me. I'm starved." Katelyn got her food and sat down at the table. Rachel had begun clearing the dishes away.

"Max, this is terrific!" Katelyn said, after taking a bite. "The salad's good, too."

"Thank you."

"No, thank you for cooking for us."

"I enjoy cooking, so that's not a problem," Max

said. "Sometimes it's hard to find people to eat with." He glanced at Mom, who smiled.

"I think we can help you out with that," Rachel said, plopping down beside her sister.

"How about a game of four-handed cribbage?" Katelyn asked. "Since you're all just sitting around watching me eat anyway?"

Rachel was already reaching for the cards and the cribbage board.

"Sure," Max said.

Mom nodded. Katelyn could see she was pleased. "Me and Max against Mom and Rachel," she said.

"You haven't got a hope," Rachel said, confident as ever.

Katelyn thought her sister was wrong there. Hope was one thing she did have.

Acknowledgments

Thank you to Levi Miller, Herald Press editor (now retired), for encouraging me to write this story and affirming that it was a "strong sequel."

I am also grateful to attorneys David Stutsman and Phil Zimmerman for sharing their knowledge to help me understand the legal processes as they relate to this novel. Thank you, Patricia Harrison Easton for providing editorial expertise.

I deeply appreciate all my friends and family who read this as the story unfolded. Special thanks—for encouragement and insights—to Deb Hartman, Shari Kammerdiener, Gouri Kumaran, my daughter Anya Stucky, my mother Marilyn Klassen, my sister-in-law Mary Klassen, Deb Handrich, Madalyn Metzger, Chad Horning, Susan Miller, Gayle Frey, Mick Sommers, Steve Garboden, and Rhonda Yoder. (This is not a complete list, so forgive me if your name also belongs on this list, and I've forgotten to include you.)

**FIRST MENNONITE CHURCH
RICHMOND, VA**

The Author

Kirsten L. Klassen has been writing fiction in her free time for many years. She holds a master's degree in business and technical communication, and earns her living as a professional writer. She lives in Northern Indiana with her daughter. Her first novel, *Katelyn's Affection*, was published by Herald Press in 2004. This is her second novel.

Made in the USA
Charleston, SC
19 February 2012